ZERO HOURS

CW00687745

Saskia McCracken is based in Glasgow, Editor at Osmosis Press, and a member of 12 Collective and the Victoria Writers' Circle. Her publications include *Imperative Utopia* (-algia press), *The King of Birds* (Hickathrift Press), *Cyanotypes* (Dancing Girl Press), and *Common Name* (Osmosis Press). She won the *Floresta* poetry prize, came second in the Streetcake Experimental Fiction Prize, was shortlisted for the Future Places Environmental Essay Prize, and longlisted for The Nature Chronicles Prize and Bath Flash Fiction Prize. Her writing has appeared in *Datableed*, *Magma*, *Amberflora*, *Hungry Ghost*, and *Zarf*, and been anthologized by Dostoyevsky Wannabe and SPAM Press.

ISBN: 978-1-915079-50-3

Cover designed by Katrina Falco

Edited and typeset by Aaron Kent

Broken Sleep Books
Rhydwen
Talgarreg
Ceredigion
SA44 4HB

Broken Sleep Books
Fair View
St George's Road
Cornwall
PL26 7YH

Zero Hours

Saskia McCracken

Also by Saskia McCracken

The King of Birds	(Hickathrift Press, 2022)
Cyanotypes	(Dancing Girl Press, 2022)
Imperative Utopia	(-algia press, 2021)

Contents

for Eadie, Lucy and Ki,
who helped me start these
stories, and for Greg who
helped me finish them

Call Centre

One day she woke up without a body. Only it wasn't really waking up, if you didn't have a body, she thought. Only it wasn't really thinking, either. But it was like waking up. That moment where you feel conscious but can't grasp the immediate past. She knew what waking up felt like because she'd had a body, once.

Once she had been a voice in an answering machine.

Good afternoon you've reached [insert business name]. There's no one available to take your call at the moment. Please leave a message and someone will get back to you as soon as possible.

There's no one available. There is no one. Bad grammar, that, she had once thought, reading the script.

Because, once, she could read, and had been part voice, part body, part machine. Ears crushed against her head by a headset, and the wire between the headset and the monitor was an umbilical cord that was cut every evening and she was born. Or was it the spine that held together her organic and machine parts, and her voice wrapped around that cord, that spine, like flesh? Once, she didn't like it when people compared the wire to an umbilical cord or a spine. Bad metaphors, or similes, depending on if they said 'like' or not. Because once, she was not a cyborg, she was a woman in a call centre twirling the cable that ran between her headset and the monitor, and it was not umbilical or a spine, it was just a wire.

Good morning/afternoon [insert accordingly] Inga speaking, how can I help? (How *may* I help you?) I'm afraid he's out of office at the moment, can (may) I take a message and ask him to call you back? What is your name please? How do you spell that please? What company are you calling from please? Could you spell that for me please? What is your phone number please? Could you repeat that please? What is your mother's maiden name, could you spell that for me please? Do you have any allergies, what are they please? What was your worst fear as a child, could you describe that for me please? What do you feel when you look at yourself naked in the

9

mirror, could you describe that feeling for me please? When did you last floss your teeth? What would you like me to ask you? Can you tell if I'm human or not please? I am. Not I'm (she edited the script). I am.

Once she had been unemployed, and she had told people she'd rather be on the dole than a cog in the machine. And then she was on the dole and she changed her mind. Bouncing payments and pot noodle, ketchup sandwiches made from stolen sachets; cards declined and meter keys with blinking lights; sellotaping the letterbox shut only to find the waves of envelopes lapping at the other side of the door, and wading through them in the hallway in wellingtons, and that was more embarrassing than removing the Sellotape. And the letters always said Dear Inga, and always spelled her surname wrong.

Once she had been a teenage girl with too much pocket money and picked pockets anyway. Or not enough pocket money, or none, or had been raised by au pairs, or had this or that or the other kind of childhood.

Once she had been caught drinking sea water, it tasted good and she had wet sand stuck to burnt skin, cold wind blew burning, and the water tasted like olives and the smell of seaweed, she had shiny blue nail varnish on her toenails, sand-scraped, and broken shells she had skin she had a body. Once. But. Once she had woken up, once she was without a body, and couldn't wake up and couldn't sleep in a paper tent to cover her, otherwise naked beneath the baking thirsty sun she could not burn, she could not taste sea water anymore.

Direct Marketing

Duncan was interviewed in the basement of a converted townhouse in the city centre. He sat opposite a panel of three people. The man on the panel was wearing a suit that looked like his, bought in Primark. The two women were wearing strong perfume and one woman had lip-gloss that made little strings between her upper and lower lip when her mouth was partly open, as she wrote things down. She didn't ask him anything. She just took notes. The other woman was in charge. She spent the interview leaning towards him with her hands clasped on the table, looking straight at him. Whenever he looked away and back again, she was looking at him. The man asked him if he felt that he had leadership qualities, if he had ambitions to manage his own team one day. Duncan said yes. She asked him where he saw himself in five years' time. He said, sitting in your seat. They looked impressed. They asked what his strengths and weaknesses were. He said his strength was team leadership and his weakness was obsessive attention to detail. The other woman continued taking notes.

They told him that every member of staff that they hired had the fantastic opportunity to become the manager of the next branch that they were opening. They preferred people with no experience. That way, they could train them according to the company standards without coming up against any bad sales habits. They told him the role was Direct Marketing. Nothing like door-to-door sales. No. That was a thing of the past. Direct Marketing meant bringing the product to the potential client, and developing a face-to-face connection with them. There was quick career progression. Competitive pay meant that the job was commission only. There was no basic pay. They found that people worked harder and produced better results when this safety net wasn't holding them back. There were also prizes if you sold lots of things. First, you had to prove that you had NSF – Natural Sales Flair.

They called Duncan the day after the interview to say that, after much consideration, he was one of the lucky few that had made it to the next stage. At the training and assessment day, they took him out on a job so that he could observe and learn from one of the senior Direct Marketers in action. He met Rory outside the building where he'd had his interview. Rory was wearing a Primark suit like him, and like the man on the interview panel. Rory had cufflinks with pearls on them. He was saving up for his wedding, and had won several prizes at work, including a flat screen TV. They walked from the building to the bus stop and waited, while Rory told him that the company had changed his life, and that he had started right at the bottom and worked his way up. Everybody did. It was all based on how good you were at Direct Marketing, nothing else mattered.

It started snowing. They got on the bus to Castlemilk shopping centre, and he asked Rory what happened if no one bought anything. Rory said that of course it wouldn't make sense for the company to pay them unless they were making sales. Today Duncan would watch Rory selling meter keys. These keys were a fantastic deal, Rory said, a total bargain. Usually, a big electric company charged a flat daily rate on their meter key and would charge extra if you used more electricity than they deemed standard. So you were being charged for electricity even if you didn't use any. This meter key was pay-as-you-go, but with no flat rate. You only paid for what you used, at a slightly higher rate than the big companies, sure, but only for what you used.

They got off at the shopping centre and sat down in the Greggs, where Rory gave him some paperwork to fill in. Rory treated him to a cup of tea and a sausage roll. Duncan ticked the relevant Equal Opportunities boxes, and wrote down his personal details. He wrote long answers to questions about why he was perfect for the role. As he wiped crumbs off the forms, they left little stains of grease on the paper.

Then Rory asked him to stand beside him at the entrance of the shopping centre and observe his technique. It was a Tuesday morning. No one came in or out. Rory straightened his tie. He held a clipboard in one arm, and a meter key in his other hand. After a while, Rory began swinging the meter key on its keyring, round and around his finger. They walked up and down in front of the entrance. The automatic entrance doors opened and closed as they walked, and flurries of snow drifted in.

Lavender

They were cleaning the en suite bedrooms on the seventh floor of the hotel. Deidre was doing one side of the corridor and her daughter Mary the other. When they got to the last room at the end, Deidre said, how about we do this one together? They rolled their cleaning trolleys in, one after another, and closed the door. Deirdre put her finger over her lips and turned on the Hoover.

She left it standing there in front of the bed and they went into the bathroom. She put the plug in the bath and turned on both taps, the hot on full blast, the cold just a little bit. Now, she said, pouring a half empty bottle of bath oils and a full bottle of bubble bath into the water, – nothing but the best for my girls. She patted Mary's belly and left her by the bath, closing the door behind her. Mary heard the drone of the Hoover moving over the carpet, the clink of bottles from the mini bar. Her mother would be picking up wads of used tissues, knickers from the floor, putting them in the bin.

Mary took off her uniform, hung her dress, tights and apron on the back of the door, placed her shoes by the mirror, and climbed into the bath. She felt water tingling hot over her skin, piled bubbles over her belly, felt the rush of blood back to her feet as she inched her toes above the water at the other end, nail varnish pink and chipped.

Deirdre was singing –

> I am a poor young girl that's straight from Cappoquin,
> I'm in search of Lord Gregory, pray God I'll find him.
>
> The rain beats my yellow locks and the dew wets me still,
> My babe is cold in my arms, Lord Gregory, let me in.
>
> Lord Gregory, he's not here and henceforth can't be seen,
> For he's gone to bonny Scotland to bring home his new queen.

> So leave now these windows and likewise this hall,
> For it's deep in the sea you should hide your downfall.

Deidre piled the dirty linen next to her trolley and changed the pillowcases. There was the snap of a new sheet thrown over the bed.

> But who will shoe my babe's little feet? Who'll put gloves
> on her hand?
> Who will tie my babe's middle with a long linen band?
>
> Who will comb my babe's yellow hair with an ivory comb?
> Who will be my babe's father till Lord Gregory comes home?
>
> Do you recall, darling Gregory, that night in Cappoquin?
> When we both changed pocket handkerchiefs and me
> against my will?
>
> For yours was pure linen, love, and mine but coarse cloth,
> For yours cost a guinea, love, and mine but one groat.

There were bubbles in Mary's hair and the smell of lavender. She remembered that smell from the sheets on the line in the tenement courtyard where she used to play, where she used to sit in the washing basket.

> Do you remember, love Gregory, that night in Cappoquin?
> We changed rings on our fingers and me against my will.
>
> For yours was pure silver, love, and mine was but tin,
> For yours cost a guinea, love, and mine but one cent.

Her mother, spraying the surfaces in the next room, was there with her in the courtyard twelve years ago. Deidre wore a yellow dress and denim jacket, and was pegging towels, sheets, odd socks on the line with a cigarette in her mouth, smelling of smoke and lavender.

Now my curse on you, Mother, my curse being so
I dream the girl I love came a-knocking at my door.

Sleep down, you foolish son, sleep down and sleep on
For its long ago that weary girl lies drowning in the sea.

Smelling of smoke and lavender, Mary sat in the washing basket. Her brother pulled her around the courtyard, barking. They were Arctic explorers, her brother a husky sled team. The wind blew the bright socks on the line. A blizzard. The tenements rose around them, icebergs, a snowstorm of bedsheets. Deidre dragged on her cigarette, humming a ballad.

Then saddle me the black horse, the brown and the bay,
Come saddle me the best horse in my stable today.

And I'll range over mountains, over valleys so wide
Till I find the girl I love, and I'll lay by her side.

Mary slept in that washing basket as a baby, and her brother before her. Now she rested her hands on her belly. Her baby would have a cradle, white, that you could rock gently, with yellow drapes. She would buy them herself. She lay in the scented bubbles, the sound of her mother spraying furniture polish in the next room. Mary would call her baby Lavender.

Bar Tender

Bar Tender:	Morning Alan, usual? Miserable day isn't it?
Alan:	(nods)
Bar Tender:	Pint of Tennent's coming up.
Alan:	
Bar Tender:	Been up to much Alan?
Alan:	(shakes head)
Bar Tender:	Nah, me either. Same old same old. Lots of uni work.
Alan:	
Bar Tender:	
Alan:	
Bar Tender:	Been reading this play for drama group tomorrow. It's called *Night, Mother*, you know it?
Alan:	(shakes head)
Bar Tender:	Well it's pretty bleak. Most of the reading is pretty bleak. It's about a woman who is going to kill herself, and her mother is trying to persuade her not to, but she does it anyway.
Alan:	
Bar Tender:	Makes you wonder what her childhood was like, the daughter. Another pint?
Alan:	(nods)
Bar Tender:	Coming up. My childhood was pretty uneventful. Feel a bit like I'm still a child really, living with Mum. She did her best though, and I don't think I've turned out too bad. But no one does I suppose. She used to love brushing my hair – here you go – and she was pretty upset when I cut it off.
Alan:	(nods)
Bar Tender:	Really miserable weather. Still, we can always count on you to come in. Ah, here's Graham. Morning Graham, the usual?
Graham:	(unfolding wet newspaper) Aye.

Bar tender:	Here you go then, one Deuchars in your special tankard.
Graham:	(reading) Thanks.
Alan:	
Bar Tender:	Talkative bunch today aren't we? I normally can't get a word in edgeways.
Alan:	
Bar Tender:	Ah, must be the football. Did we lose, Alan? I had the night off yesterday and never found out the score. Heard loads of chanting and the street was full of plastic cups and empty bottles this morning though. I was watching Strictly with Mum. No football allowed. I was telling her about the play and about how you never find out anything really, about the daughter's childhood. You're thirsty today, aren't you? Another pint?
Alan:	(nods)
Bar Tender:	You must've seen a lot growing up around here. What was your childhood like Alan?
Alan:	Short.

Scenes

Zero Hour life is too prosaic for poetry. Just polishing glasses, cutlery, taking orders, carrying plates, wiping tables. No cigarette breaks, paid breaks, line breaks. There are too many things that don't happen for any kind of biography or memoir. You can only go over the finer details of a customer complaint for so long before you realise that no one is listening. The exception is more interesting than the rule. The rule is that lots of us do this work. The rule is that these contracts are convenient for some and not for most. The rule is that the thing everyone says will happen – the dramatic moment you quit because you've finally had enough – doesn't happen. You'll speak your mind to the customer or the manager. You probably won't. And the shifts patterns don't create the structure and space and narrative arc that a novel might demand. You have too much time or not enough time and when you have too much time, you're looking for other work so no time, really, for a novel. What form does zero hour life demand? Zero Hours means what your careers advisor calls a Portfolio Career, a collage of sketches, scraps, pieced together in the off hours or the on hours. On notepads in different coloured inks because your pens keep disappearing. On paper that sticks with beer or gravy. On texts to yourself during a cigarette break you're not allowed. The lives of the obscure are fragmented. Waiting for phone calls that mostly don't come, four-hour shifts, long days in between, texts from agencies, emails, conversations at the bar, stories, interruptions, sketches, silences, scenes.

Spill

The one that stayed with her now, and followed her, was Lars von Trier's *Melancholia*. Watching it felt like moving slowly through thick, dark water, through – who had she cited then? – unexhausted time. Even now she heard, through the rush of voices at the bar, a submerged orchestra going over the same notes she'd written about. The sound of eco-poetic cinema, she had written, was –

But someone here was waving money at her at the end of the bar, hoping to be served before everyone else, and the man in front of her spilled his mojito and wanted another for free, as he'd not begun drinking it yet, and now it was all over his shirt front and the floor. Everyone else, crowded round waiting for their drinks, looked at him and hoped this would not mean they had to wait longer

She turned away and looked for blue roll to mop up the melting ice

Yes, she had dedicated a chapter of her book to representations of ice melting, dissolving, or thickening, spreading on screen. Of winter worlds where every sound was softened, deadened by snow and ocean and where vast bergs split the air, split apart and wolves walked over the waves

Her thesis examiner wanted to know why she had chosen big budget sci-fi films and badly reviewed horror to go alongside her work on art house cinema. Well, she said

I'm afraid we can't give you another mojito for free

And she ignored the woman waving money at her and turned to the person next to the man who had spilled the drink. What can I get for you?

But she was thinking about something to do with music, with being submerged, with slow movement, as though moving with great effort through sand maybe it was, with light dappling the water, perhaps the seabed, or a fish tank

She smacked mint to get the scent, twisted the rim of the glass in salt, put paper umbrellas and two straws in each drink. They were going to stop serving plastic straws soon, for the environment. But it wasn't straws that were the focus of what she called eco-monstrosity, eco-horror. Alex Garland's *Annihilation* sees lichen blooming from bodies, human voices screaming in the mouths of bears, the mutation of DNA in the opposite of deep time, evolution refracted by a meteor and excess beyond our control yes, beyond the end of drinking cocktails without straws

We are afraid, she said, that while we move incrementally towards and away from solutions

The man was not going to leave without a complimentary mojito. She had knocked it over, so she should replace it

She picked up the wet glass with a few pieces of crushed ice at the bottom. It was cracked. She took it to the glass bin under the sink, which was full, and took the bin, squeezing through the customers, outside to the bigger glass bin, which was also full

So, her external examiner had asked her, eco-horror had something to do with fear of excess and simultaneously, of annihilation, was that what she was trying to get at? And was she afraid, he asked, of slowness, or of its opposite? She needed to unpack, to clarify, to tease out her meaning. Was she afraid, he didn't ask, of what would happen next

It was quiet out by the bins, and she heard again the faint strains of that underwater orchestra that meant, for *Melancholia*, the inevitability of

Emptying the small glass bin into the overflowing big one, bits of broken glass and beer bottles spilled out, fell at her feet and shattered.

Potato Pancakes

Ewelina's sister was going to have a baby (Ewelina diced the onions). Her sister, who, when they were teenagers, had had that horrible incident (she took the roast potatoes out of the oven and put them on the plates next to the sprouts), yes, incident would be the English word. Her sister Julia, who had been told she would never be able to have children and who, a child herself at the time, had cried and cried, and listened to Ewelina's favourite Iron Maiden CD on repeat until they both hated it (on her way to get the gravy she stacked the oven trays that were on the side, thick with white fat, and put them by the sink).

Davey Smiles, the pot wash man, had the most gold teeth of anyone she had ever known. He never wore washing up gloves, and moisturised his hands on every cigarette break. Davey Smiles turned to the stack of trays and said – Go back to Poland hen – as he always did when she gave him something to wash. She smiled as he always expected her to smile. She was going to go back, if only for a couple of weeks. She was going to see her sister, and her sister was going to have a baby. (She poured the gravy over the roast dinners and the waiter whisked the plates away).

In those Iron Maiden days, Ewelina cooked. She cooked her sister lots of things, but the only thing Julia would eat were potato pancakes. They weren't like the potato scones people had with a full Scottish breakfast here. Here potato scones were little fried brown triangles that tasted like salt and oil. No. In those days, before Scotland, Ewelina had peeled and grated the potatoes, and rinsed them thoroughly. She did the same to two small onions and crushed some garlic. Then she mixed the ingredients together with one egg yolk (beaten stiff), red peppers, and some flour, throwing in thick pinches of salt and pepper, and knotting in parsley. Julia would be blasting '666 the Number of the Beast' at full volume while their grandmother banged on the bedroom door, shouting, coaxing, pleading.

Ewelina would drop spoonsful of the mixture into a hissing frying pan, then press them gently with the spatula. She did everything gently, quietly, quickly. When they were crisp and browned, she patted them with kitchen roll. The rule was to eat them with mayonnaise and dill, but Julia was obsessed with ketchup. So Ewelina carried up her offering with a bottle of Heinz. The bedroom door would open just long enough for her to slip through with the plate, her grandmother stuck outside. Then the two of them would sit on the floor, listening to that horrible CD and eating potato pancakes covered in ketchup. When their grandmother found out she was horrified. How could anyone aspire to be a chef and use ketchup on potato pancakes? This was not America.

Yes, she had aspired, even then. Because of then, maybe. The two seemed to be the same to her, the aspiring days and those Iron Maiden days. But her thoughts were interrupted by Duncan, the head waiter who collected foreign swear words and chat-up lines. One of the customers on table four was gluten intolerant. Could they have one of the gluten-free buns with their soup please? *Prosím*?

Ewelina served up the bun. As he took it, she said, without thinking – my sister is going to have a baby.

Cool, Duncan said, *wunderbar*, and walked off to table four.

She paused, leaning against the counter and looking out into the restaurant. Gluten free? Her grandmother said it was an invention. And who invented it? Ewelina had asked.

The – what do you call them? Her grandmother said. Young people created allergies so they'd have something to complain about. But still Julia said she wasn't going to eat gluten while she was pregnant, just in case.

Pregnant, eh? Davey Smiles shouted as he scrubbed the fat off the oven trays. What are you going to do to celebrate? You have baby showers over there? And what about tonight?

Ewelina turned around. He was grinning. All his front teeth were gold. (She started plating up the mains, two chicken, three beef, one vegetarian roast).

Vodka and gherkins is it? Davey Smiles said.

That was the last order, she said. Kitchen's closed. Time to start cleaning up.

Get tae fuck, he said. You're not celebrating? You've got to celebrate.

They cleaned everything but one hob, one sideboard. They scraped plates and put them in the pot wash. Bones and gravy-browned vegetables piled above the top of the food bin. The waiters all went home, except for Duncan, who wanted to talk to the manager about becoming a supervisor. (Ewelina took one egg, a few potatoes and onions, garlic, peppers, flour and parsley. She greased one skillet.)

I'll clean these last bits, she said. You can go home if you want.

What are you doing? Davey Smiles asked.

I'm going back to Poland next week for a bit.

I didnae mean it like that, he said. I didnae mean you should actually leave. I mean, what are you cooking?

It's for my sister, she said. I'm celebrating.

What are these then eh? He gestured towards her with a sponge as she grated the potatoes.

You'll see, she said.

You'd better let me have some and aw, he said.

He stacked the clean plates and put away the pans. He left the clean cutlery in buckets for the staff on the next shift to polish. He sprayed and wiped down the surfaces. He swept. Duncan and the manager left. Ewelina had the keys for lock-up. She was scooping her mix into the skillet, in little blobs, and flattening them. Davey watched as he mopped the kitchen floor. When they were brown and crispy, she patted the potato cakes gently with kitchen roll and offered him the plate.

Is this Polish food then? He said. Looks a bit like hash browns. I bet they'd be good with ketchup, eh?

Mixology

Duncan was a master of serviette origami, of twirling cocktail-ripe bottles of raspberry puree into pink Bellinis, of flaming rum passion fruit halves, afloat/stranded/run aground on crushed ice. He was an artist, magician, entertainer. He was a man whose waistcoat pockets were heavy as chainmail at the end of the night, chinking with coins. People who didn't tip him were the exception. He thanked them in every possible language. Thank you, thanks, muchos gracias, merci, merci beaucoup, grazie mille, arigato, do jeh, daw-dyeh, vielen Dank, khop khun kha, spasiba, gamsahabnida, takk, mahalo, toda, efharisto, dziękuję ci, dank je wel, cheers mate etc. etc. etc. He picked up new words as he went. His Bloody Marys were strong enough to make you weep. Guaranteed. The only person immune from Duncan's Bloody Mary effect was Davey Smiles, and he probably didn't have any taste buds. Duncan had made the manager cry with the heat. Poor Massimo.

Checkout

Sometimes Dierdre would say hello without looking at the customer until she had checked out three items and guessed, based on those items, what the person would be like. At first, she was quite confident in her guesses:

Option 1.   Avocado, rye bread, oat milk = hipster
Option 2.   Tea, milk, bread = someone normal, like her
Option 3.   Spaghetti hoops, white sliced bread, own brand butter = someone down on their luck
Option 4.   Pot noodle, gravy, vodka = student
Option 5.   Coke, crisps, chocolate = school child
Option 6.   Tampons, rosé, pain killers = young woman
Option 7.   Buckfast, beer, burgers = young man
Option 8.   Rice, noodles, soy sauce = international student

When she spoke to her son, Duncan, after he got back from work at the hotel, she told him her trio of things and asked him to guess who'd bought them. He would laugh if it was a stereotype of a student or hipster, and would become embarrassed if it was someone down on their luck or foreign. He would tell her, punch up, not down, Ma.

But she soon realised, not because of Duncan, but because of the unpredictability of people's purchases, that her game didn't work. The local lads drank rosé, the students ate crumpets, the hipsters liked spaghetti hoops and the international students bought Buckfast. People's baskets and trolleys overflowed with the most random combinations. She was forced to change her game.

The new game was to see who spent more money, men or women. But often men and women shopped together, and even paid together. Then it became, who drank more alcohol? But that was rather depressing, because it turned out that once you started counting units, a lot of people drank a lot more alcohol than was good for them. Same went for fizzy drinks and sweets. Then it was, who had the worst period – did they buy tampons with chocolate, wine, painkillers, or gin? Then it was, who spent the most money, then who spent the least.

Then management introduced a new game – who could work the fastest. The winner got a free bottle of red, the runners up got nothing, and the slowest people lost their jobs. Only the management didn't tell them about the last bit, and if Deirdre had complained about it, they would have said it was nothing to do with the game. People were losing their jobs because they were being replaced by technology. You only needed one member of staff per eight self-service checkout machines. But Deirdre knew that the game and the technology were connected. She eyed the competition. Only two people were older than her: Edith and Alastair.

Edith was very old. She claimed she had driven ambulances in the war, and then fire engines down in London. She had lost her job when her eyesight became too bad for driving, and moved back up to Scotland. Her glasses were thick as the base of a whisky tumbler. Edith took the competition (because she knew it wasn't a game) very seriously. She would start ringing through the next customer's purchases before the first customer had put their wallet away. She would have spare till roll waiting by the machine, just in case it ran out. In quiet spells, she would restock on plastic bags, change the till rolls even if they hadn't run out, and push all the dividers that people put on the conveyor belt within easy customer reach. She always seemed to have more dividers and more plastic bags than anyone else.

Alastair was about Deirdre's age. He had been a stay-at-home father and never qualified to do anything else. His wife was rich, ran a betting shop. Their children were grown up now, were older than Duncan. Alasdair didn't like the game, but he played as well as he could. The trouble was, he was always asking people how their day was, and sometimes they would stand there chatting until the customers in the queue behind complained. Then, sometimes, an argument would start, and it would take ages before anyone left. Alastair's till always had the longest queue, the sort you'd avoid.

The rest of the team were younger than Deirdre. Some were students, some were foreigners, the rest were mothers whose children were either in school or grown up. Some of them were chatty, but all of them were faster than she was. And she couldn't blame it on age. Edith won the game. Nobody was surprised. She took home a bottle of Chateau Neuf du Pape. About a month later, when the management thought everyone had forgotten about the game, they started letting the slowest people go. Milly, who never stopped talking, Marie, whose English wasn't very good, Dirk, who spent most of his time stocking shelves and avoiding the tills, Lionel, who was a bit of a pervert in Deirdre's opinion (always going after Milly), Alastair, who went back to being a househusband, and Deirdre.

Let go. As though management had been clinging onto them while they begged for release. Why couldn't they just say fired, like they used to? Redundant. That was even worse. As though she had nothing of value to offer them whatsoever. But the worst thing was that she still had to shop there, because it was the only supermarket near her house, and she wasn't going to spend money on a bus to the second closest supermarket on point of pride.

A few weeks later she joined the agency Duncan was working for, and got a cleaning job doing hotels and offices, as and when, wherever she was needed. The pay was minimum wage, but combined with her pension, it was enough to start a new game.

So she did. She would go and buy only two items at a time, and pick Edith's queue, or any of the supervisors' tills, depending on what mood she was in. She never used the self-service checkout machines. Then she would buy her paired items and watch their faces closely for a reaction. The more offensive the better. The more embarrassed they were the more satisfied she would feel. Afterwards, she'd call up Duncan and tell him of her latest purchase, and about how shocked the supervisors were. If it was anything morbid, he laughed, if it was sexual, he'd groan with embarrassment, if it was racist he'd remind her, punch up not down, Ma.

Day 1.   Baby food and vodka.
Day 2.   Dog food and rat poison.
Day 3.   Toilet paper and anti-diuretics.
Day 4.   Sleeping tablets and razor blades.
Day 5.   Condoms and pineapple juice.
Day 6.   A multi-coloured Halloween afro wig and shoe polish.
Day 7.   Bleach and lettuce.
Day 8.   A pregnancy test and a single coat hanger.

Zero Logic

In your contract, you agree that your employer is not obliged to secure you any work at all, and you are not obliged to accept and work any of the shifts that your employer does offer you. You might have a week with no work (and no pay) because your employer says there aren't any shifts available – i.e., the agency that employs you has not secured any contracts for shifts you could work that week. No one, no hotels, sports stadiums, performance arenas etc., are holding any events that require your services. Anyone who signs a Zero Hour contract knows this.

Some weeks there's loads of work, some weeks there's none. This is why most people have contracts with two or three agencies. They're hoping to maximise the selection of shifts available. Even though you've been told that you have a shift and that you'll get paid a minimum of four hours work (on the minimum wage) if you turn up, this does not always happen. When you turn up you are turned away from your shift and sent home, without being compensated for your travel expenses. Reasons for being turned away fall into several categories:

Grooming

You are a woman wearing a woman's shirt, instead of the standard, 'neutral' shirt from the men's section of Primark.

Or.

Your sleeves are too short (e.g. three quarter length), your shirt doesn't do up to your chin, it is tailored or tapered at the waist, it has frills, it is the wrong colour or dirty, it has not been ironed, it is the wrong size and does not tuck in, or it does not have a collar for your tie.

Or.

You have forgotten to bring your tie. If there is a Primark nearby and you are fast, you may be encouraged to run over to buy a tie, at your own expense, to work the shift you signed up for.

The tie is too skinny, or wide, or short, or shiny. It is the wrong colour. It is a bow tie not a Windsor. It has an inappropriate pattern, avocados, cats, Christmas trees.

Or.

Your trousers are not long enough (e.g. three quarter length), or are not deemed formal, 'smart black dress trousers' because: they have a decorative feature e.g. frills or quirky pockets; they are not 'smart' material i.e. they are silk, cotton, or linen; they are not black; they feature a pattern (such as pin-stripes); they have not been ironed.

Or.

Your socks are not black and/or do not cover your ankles.

Or.

Your shoes are not smart enough e.g. trainers, boots, heels, converse, etc., or are too shiny e.g. PVC, or too matt e.g. suede, or don't comply with health and safety regulations e.g. peep-toe or sandals. You have coloured shoelaces. Shoes must be smart, black, clean, and polished.

Your hair must be tied back neatly and pinned/sprayed in place where necessary. If you don't have a hairband or your hair is messy, or your hair is 'too Afro', or if your face is not clean shaven, go home.

If you are deemed shabby but salvageable, the agency staff may: tell you to apply deodorant; put pins in your hair without asking you, and fix any flyaway locks with hairspray; polish your shoes; tell you to shave your face if is a razor is available; tell you to wear more or less make-up; tell you to remove all piercings (excluding wedding bands and including tongue bars, cuff piercings, nose studs etc.); send you home if you're wearing nail varnish even if it is transparent;

tell you to tuck in your shirt; tell you to remove and iron your shirt if an iron is available.

So that's grooming.

But there are other reasons that you may not get the work you've been promised.

Overbooks

You are an 'overbook'. An overbook means the agency has promised the hotel/stadium/other venue, a total of, say, fifteen members of staff (waiters/bar staff) for the day. The agency assumes several people will confirm that they can work and then won't turn up for this shift. Therefore, the agency tells twenty staff members to turn up, although they know that the hotel/stadium/whatever will only pay for fifteen members of staff. If every single one of those twenty people turns up, five will be sent home. Usually these are the last five to turn up. Also, if you are not an overbook, but you are late, they will offer your shift to an overbook. Don't be late.

Or the hotel/stadium/whatever realise that even though they've asked for fifteen staff members, they are now expecting fewer customers than they first estimated, and so correspondingly, they only need ten members of staff, for example. So ten of the twenty agency staff that turn up are sent home unpaid.

Other Reasons

The shift is cancelled at the last minute.

You are late.

Or.

It may also be the case that you're told your shift will be eight hours long. But while you're working your manager decides that they don't really need you. It's not very busy. Having staff walking around with nothing to do costs money and looks bad. They're contractually obliged to pay you a minimum of four hours work, now that you've started. So you're guaranteed less that £40 (regardless of age) once you start. Therefore, they keep you until those four hours are over, even if there's nothing to do. Maybe they'll have you polishing plates, or glasses, or cutlery. Maybe you'll be folding napkins into triangles. Maybe you'll be cleaning. As soon as the four hours are done, they send you home.

Rear-View Mirror

So much happens beyond the edges of the mirror. Conversations without faces. Voices and silences. Sometimes eye contact in the glass. How's your night going? Busy shift? But most do not. Nights are best. Nights are worst. So many small worlds. Like a mussel seen through the crack where the

shell splits before you break it open. This is a between time; always between places; other people's destinations, futures. There are things you can do and say when everything is paused. Rules belong to places and you are not there yet. Rules are for faces and you can't see mine. An eyebrow, an eye, half

a nose, half my lips. And you, only an elbow, a knee, a handbag, a small dog perhaps. Tans, tattoos, football t-shirts, beards, flags, placards. LCOME OME or LACK IVES TTER. A bottle of wine, a bookcase. Rucksacks and wheelie cases. Children who won't sit down. Takeaway boxes in plastic bags

with the handles tied. Or the smell of vinegar as chips spill onto the floor. Sometimes the mirror is filled with flowers and fingers. Or heels in hands, dangling by the straps, bare feet on seats. Outside the frame are all the things I'll find afterwards: earrings, empty cans, food trodden into the floor, paper bags full of wrapped gifts, handbags, coats, beer bottles, umbrellas,

wallets, scarves, backpacks, unused tampons, sunglasses, single gloves, women's shoes, tights, empty condom wrappers, five-pound notes, train tickets, boarding passes, lipstick, polaroid photos, the smell of perfume. A young woman asleep, hair covering her face, an empty champagne bottle held loosely in her hand. No bubbles left. Snoring. But it isn't afterwards often.

Virtual Reception

Astrid was a week into the job when she found out that the hotel had burned down the previous autumn. It was now May.

In April, she had woken up each day at 8am, put on a full face of make-up, and waited for the admin temping agency to call. Her shirt, blazer, and pencil skirt were ironed and ready. When, by 10am, she had not received a call, she would remove her make-up and job hunt in the long afternoons in her pyjamas. Between each job application she would binge watch old episodes of Ru Paul's Drag Race and eat bowls of couscous with basil flavoured Dolmio sauce. Sometimes she had a Cornetto for dessert. In the evenings she cleaned the flat. When there was nothing left to Hoover and no surface areas left to wipe down, and nothing left to bleach, she scrubbed the oven, cleaned out the inside of the fridge, cleaned behind the fridge. She washed the windows and mirrors. She wiped dust off the leaves of her spider plant, Simon, and sprayed him with water.

Then one morning they called. Could she be at Blythswood Offices at 9am for training? She could. Astrid was going to be a receptionist for three weeks, covering someone on holiday. Her contact, Josephine, met her at the front door of the office wearing a pink dress and blazer, and took her into a room full of desks. Every desk had two monitors and a headset. The other women in the room were younger than Astrid. They were talking into their headsets and looking at their monitors. Josephine took her to her desk and showed her the laminated step-by-step instruction sheet for taking calls. They were all virtual receptionists, Josephine said. There were over four hundred businesses registered at this address. Anyone who called these businesses got through to one of the women on the headsets. There were eight of them, including Astrid, who were expected to answer the phone in twelve rings or less.

One monitor had a spreadsheet with all the details of the businesses and how each one required you to answer the phone. For example, Good Morning/Good Afternoon, Terry's Tiles, how can I help you today? I'm afraid Terry is unavailable at the moment, can I please take a message?

The other monitor was open on an email account, where Astrid had to contact the business owner with the caller's message, and their contact details. She also had to log all her calls manually as she was taking them, in a logbook. It was simple once you got used to it. You just had to be quick and efficient.

She took calls on behalf of Terry's Tiles, a home-visit beauty salon, a window cleaning company, a sexual therapy helpline, a carpet sales company that never seemed to deliver any carpets (she had lots of complaints), and lots of plumbers and construction workers. She logged her calls and sent her emails. She answered the phone in under twelve rings most of the time.

On her lunch break, she went down into the basement with half the team and they ate their packed lunches in front of the TV. Usually they watched Dinner Dates, but once there was a reality show on about evictions, so they watched that instead. As they ate their lunch, they talked about how embarrassing the people on the shows were, how they dressed, how they behaved. There was always one person on Dinner Dates who was too keen, or too sleazy, or too picky. No one in the basement would want to go on a date with them. Then after lunch, they went back up to work and the other half of the team went downstairs.

She did lots of tea runs to get a break from the calls. Once, while she was looking out of the window between calls, she saw a man in chef whites smoking in the alley outside. Another man stumbled into the alley and started speaking to him. She watched them as she took her next call.

Good afternoon, Glaze Days, how can I help you today?

The two men seemed to be arguing. The chef was shaking his head, and the other man was swaying in front of him, shouting. He was tall, the man shouting, and very thin. His clothes were too big for him, and his shoes were undone. He tripped and stumbled into the chef. The chef pushed him away, yelled something.

I'm afraid Jordan is unavailable at the moment; can I please take a message?

The chef disappeared through the door opposite her in the alley, probably back to the kitchen.

> Good afternoon, Glasgow Furniture Repairs, how can I help you today?

The thin man leaned into the doorway. Then he jerked back and fell over. The chef was back, shouting and waving a meat cleaver over him.

Sorry could you repeat that please? I'm afraid I'll have to put you on hold, one moment please. Josephine, are you seeing this?

Everyone was looking out of the window. No one said anything. The thin man half walked, half crawled down the alley, the chef following him with the cleaver, out of sight. She looked around the room at the women all staring out of the window in their headsets. The phones rang. Josephine told them to get back to work, nothing to see here. So the hum of voices began again, the clicking of keyboards and turning of logbook pages. The chef walked back up the alley and disappeared through the door opposite, holding the cleaver loosely.

> Good afternoon, the Classic Curtain Company, how can I help you today?
> Good afternoon, Glasgow Electrics, how can I help you today?
> Good afternoon, Nightingale Clinic, how can I help you today?
> Good afternoon, McGregor and Orr Construction, how can I help you today?
> Good afternoon, Carpets of Arabia, how can I help you today?

Days passed. Dinner Dates had predictable outcomes. The food that looked delicious was delicious, the food that looked vile was vile. If it was too vile the date was ruined. If the meal was a laughable failure things sometimes worked out. If everything was excellent the staff in the basement were disappointed. They wanted drama. They wanted to be cooked an exquisite three course meal. Their sandwiches looked sadder than ever. Calls were taken. Emails were sent. Calls were logged. Tea was made. They looked out of the window. Sometimes the chef stood outside the door smoking. They saw no one else.

> Good afternoon, Seeds for Soil Solutions, how can I help you today?
> Good afternoon, Glasgow Glass and Tiles, how can I help you today?
> Good afternoon, Eternity Health, how can I help you today?
> Good afternoon, The Auld Wine Company, how can I help you today?
> Good afternoon, The Heavenly Highland Hotel, how can I help you today?

Someone called to say that they had arrived at the Heavenly Highland Hotel and found it closed, the exterior blackened, the windows blown out. There must have been a mistake, he hoped. He had paid for a double room with en-suite for three nights already, and had specifically chosen this hotel because it said it was wheelchair accessible on the website. He was outside the hotel, in his wheelchair, with his wife and all their bags. He wanted to know if he had the right address, what had happened, where he was supposed to go.

She put him on hold. She explained the situation to Josephine, who said she'd received a few calls like that about the hotel, and that it was probably best to take a message.

But what about the couple waiting? Astrid asked.

That was not their responsibility, Josephine said.

Astrid kept them on hold. She Googled the hotel. She skimmed over the headlines. Burnt down last year, they all said. Still out of use.

She told Josephine.

Well, Josephine said, tell them they can get a refund through the website where they made the booking. There's nothing else we can do about it.

But shouldn't we find them somewhere else to stay? Astrid asked. And shouldn't we report the company to the police? They shouldn't still be accepting bookings after all this time.

I'll speak to the hotel manager, Josephine said, I'm sure it's just a mistake. But there's really nothing we can do except encourage them to get a refund. If they keep talking, cut them off politely and hang up.

Astrid imagined the couple outside the burnt down hotel surrounded by bags, making their way back to wherever they'd come from. They were not pleased when she told them there was nothing she could do. They were not pleased about going onto the website for a refund. She cut him off with a thank you for calling goodbye.

Good afternoon, Mick's Motors, how can I help you today?
Good afternoon, JBC Solutions, how can I help you today?
Good afternoon, Exotic Reptiles, how can I help you today?

She had two more calls about the hotel the following week. Josephine said she'd tried, but she couldn't get hold of the hotel manager, and there was nothing else she could do about it. The manager would probably take the hotel off the website soon anyway.

We should tell the police, Astrid said again, thinking of the couple she'd cut off, stranded. She wondered if they'd found somewhere else to stay nearby, or whether they'd gone home instead. She wondered if they got their refund.

Definitely not, said Josephine. That's not our responsibility.

Whose responsibility is it then? said Astrid.

Not ours, said Josephine.

Good afternoon, the Classic Curtain Company, how can I help you today?
Good afternoon, Mick's Motors, how can I help you today?

Good afternoon, Glasgow Electrics, how can I help you today?

Good afternoon, Nightingale Clinic, how can I help you today?

Good afternoon, McGregor and Orr Construction, how can I help you today?

Good afternoon, Carpets of Arabia, how can I help you today?

Good afternoon, Terry's Tiles, how can I help you today?

Good afternoon, Eternity Health, how can I help you today?

Good afternoon, The Auld Wine Company, how can I help you today?

Good afternoon, Exotic Reptiles, how can I help you today?

Soon the three weeks were over. Astrid handed in her logbook and said goodbye to the other women. Josephine said they'd keep her on record if they needed anyone to cover shifts again. Astrid went back to her sofa, to job hunting, to couscous with basil flavoured Dolmio sauce, to Simon the spider plant, and to cleaning her flat. She felt guilty sometimes, about that couple outside the hotel, and wondered what had happened to them. She considered calling the police about the hotel but decided she probably wouldn't get called back for more work if she did. She never thought about the thin man crawling away from the chef, hunched beneath him, as he swung his cleaver.

Waiting

Because the thing with these contracts is that some days you could call up the four different agencies you're registered with and not one of them has a single shift for you. And you could call them up every day for weeks and get nothing, and then get loads of work, but all on the same day. And then you'd go with whichever shift paid most, and the other managers of the other agencies would get pissed off with you for being unavailable. So you might as well only be registered with one agency, because all of them basically just have work on at the weekends. And then you'd get four days in a row, all white shirt shifts, till 3am, and once you got home it'd be 3.30am and you'd have to wash and iron your white shirts for the next day, and spray deodorant in your beer-soaked shoes.

One of those 3.30am ironing sessions you might look out of the window and see a barefoot woman running down the empty street. And you might be too tired to see if she was ok because maybe you'd have another double shift in a few hours' time, so you'd just go straight to sleep on your sofa. In the morning you might realise it was a black shirt you needed anyway, so you didn't even need to be awake ironing your white shirts so late, so you might've slept longer, and might not have seen the woman running down the street.

And on one of those days, when there wasn't any work going and you'd already called all the agencies twice, and they'd all said there's never any shifts going in January, you might be at home watching TV. Polishing your shoes, digging cotton buds in the ridges where the vomit sticks and dries. Maybe you'd have the news on, and there'd be an exposé set on your street, the very street that you lived on, with the news presenters interviewing all the neighbours you don't know, because who meets their neighbours when you work anti-social hours? But maybe the faces would be a bit familiar, and then you could see inside people's homes where they'd be interviewed on their sofas. There were a lot of ugly sofas inside the houses on your street.

And everyone sitting on those sofas would say how they had no idea anything was going on and how the people in question had always seemed like such nice, normal people. There was always one person who got interviewed who had had an inkling from the very first, and would draw out an anecdote in a way that would make things seem very suspicious and loaded with meaning. But suppose, then, that one of your managers called, and it'd been days since your last shift. Well you'd turn off the news, wouldn't you? And forget to take down the number of the helpline for anyone who'd seen or heard anything suspicious and you wouldn't have time to report it. By the time you finished your double shift and had done your ironing there wouldn't be time to think about any of it anyway, because you'd be tired enough to fall asleep then and there on your sofa, which was a bit less ugly than the rest of the sofas on your street.

Function

Bartender: I thought I was behind the bar tonight?

Manager: The rugby guys asked for you in the function room. It'll be easy, tequila slammers all night.

Bartender: Doesn't Duncan normally do that?

Manager: They said they wanted a nice girl and pointed at you.

Bartender: And you said yes?

National Favourite

Hassan swapped shifts with Mo so that he could take his daughter and her friends to Largs, to play mini golf, for her birthday. She was ten, and he didn't know what ten-year-old girls liked (he was one of four brothers, and she was his eldest child). Her friends went to Largs every summer and she'd never been.

He didn't like swapping shifts. He had been a head chef, and he knew that they put you on a certain shift for a reason. In Karachi, he put the best chefs on at the weekend. The fact that he'd been given a Saturday shift and Mo had no weekend shifts that month probably meant that they weren't happy with Mo's work. They wouldn't be happy about them swapping shifts.

But Mo was good. He seemed odd at first, quiet, and he prayed out by the bins instead of the manager's office Hassan used. And he was thin. Never trust a thin chef, they said here. But he was a good cook, and once you got him talking that was it, you were friends. Mo had invited Hassan's family over for dinner at his house the week before. It was his first night off in ages. They had homemade Somalian food. Mo had handwritten a menu for them, and at the bottom he'd written Spaghetti Bolognese for his son, who wouldn't eat anything else.

Pan Fried Kingfish Fillet
With lemon juice and *duqus* pepper
Served with rice

Qudaar (Salad)
Tomato, onion, peas, broccoli, cabbage, celery
In a lemon and olive oil dressing

For the children:
Baasto iyo Sugo Hilib Shiidan (Spaghetti Bolognese)
With tomato, onion, garlic, and coriander

Dessert

Doolshe (Pear and Cardamom Cake)

Afterwards they had milk with cardamom. He and Mo had talked about food, what they liked to cook at home, what they thought of the menu at work, how the head chef used too much salt, whether pineapple should go on pizza (Hassan was keen, Mo was appalled). Mo told him that spaghetti was a national dish in Somalia, and how it was different in the Italian restaurants here, no coriander or cumin. Hassan must go to Mogadishu, Mo insisted, one day he must, if only for the spaghetti. They talked about the children, about what TV shows they were watching. Hassan was obsessed with home makeover shows. Mo preferred documentaries about true crime. They talked about Hassan's broken bike brakes.

Their wives had shown each other photos of home and talked about Scottish Independence, and the children, and how Scottish people always said 'pure' instead of very. The four of them talked about relatives they had in London. Fatima had a cousin who was working near London Bridge when it happened and saw the building he worked in on the news. The cousin had three sons at college. All of them had been stopped and searched over the last few years. Then the children started arguing and it was time to go home. On the way home Hassan was already planning what he would cook for Mo's family next time they were both off work.

Largs was a grey place and the beach was all stones, but the girls were excited. Fatima bought the children fish and chips and covered it all in ketchup and mayonnaise. Gulls circled and swooped at their food. One girl dropped her chips and screamed, and the gulls crowded, eating everything. Fatima bought the girl more chips. Then they all got Mr. Whippy with red sweet sauce. He liked Mr. Whippy. Fatima liked mayonnaise. They were getting used to being here.

But he couldn't understand chips. You couldn't taste the potatoes, just salt and fat. His cousin Ali was born in Scotland. Ali's father was one of the first to come over after Partition, to work as a bus driver. Hassan was surprised that Ali had a Scottish accent, even when he spoke Urdu. But then it made sense, he supposed. Ali insisted he try the local cuisine when he arrived. First, Ali treated him to a full Halal Scottish breakfast in the West End.

The following weekend they had venison, then macaroni pie. Ali thought it was all delicious. Hassan was polite about most of it but pakora was a step too far for him. What have they done to our food? he asked.

What have *we* done to our food, Ali corrected him. It's a national favourite.

That was the last of the Scottish food experiments. Hassan spent all day at work cooking mostly European dishes and that was enough for him. The mains were not to his liking. He liked the desserts. Sometimes after a shift, if it was quiet, he and Mo would sit together at the bar in their chef whites and eat puddings. They talked to the bar staff and the regulars. Football, usually.

French Martini Cheesecake (v)
Chambord Berry Compote, Pineapple Gel

Charred Peach Eton Mess (v)
Summer Fruit Compote, Toffee Sauce

Sticky Toffee Pudding (v)
Butterscotch Sauce, Salted Caramel Ice Cream

Baked Apple Tart (vg)
Berry Compote, Raspberry Sorbet, Hazelnut Crumb

But here he was, with his daughter and her friends, at Largs, eating fish and chips and Mr. Whippy in the cold, with the wind blowing bits of litter down the beach. He was about to play mini golf for the first time. They went up to the little wooden hut and paid, collecting their clubs and balls. They began with Hassan keeping score. The course was cheap and shabby with peeling blue paint on everything. He suspected that bits of the model tunnels and obstacles were missing. But he found he was good at it. He got a hole in one or two every time. He crowed over his daughter who tried to divert his ball off course. She took at least four shots every time. You have to focus, he said, aim, before you strike. She got worse. Some of the other girls were pretty good. Hassan was better. Fatima told him he should let one of the children win, but he couldn't help the fact that he was much better than the kids. Well, she said, try playing using your left side then, to make it more fair. He did. He still won.

Next week he was going to invite Mo's family for dinner. What would he make them? Perhaps he should make Mo's children something separate. Probably something mild with lots of chapati. And then a selection of dishes from home for the adults.

Although Hassan won the game of mini golf, Fatima bought one of the girls an ice cream with sprinkles on it, as a prize for getting the second-best score.

Why I don't I get an ice cream? Hassan asked.

You know why, my love, Fatima said.

They sat on the grey stony beach and watched the girls run in and out of the small waves that lapped the shore. Then the girls got bored and gathered around one of the younger ones, whose name he'd forgotten, and they all watched videos on her phone. Their son was making a pile out of some pebbles. Hassan adjusted his sitting position. The stones were digging in. He wondered if, on a clear day, you could see Ireland from here. The sea was grey like the roads and the sky. It was quiet, besides the sound of the girls' voices and the gulls crying, and the waves. Yes, he had decided what he would cook for Mo's family. He would put together a menu when he got home.

Aquarius Careers

AQUARIUS, it is time to think big and to approach career matters with confidence. If you have been out of work for a while then Jupiter's entry should see you being offered at least one opportunity to get back into the workforce.

Unfortunately

Thanks for your interest in working with Blythswood Square Offices. Unfortunately, you were unsuccessful this time but we will hold you CV on file should anything come up that suits in the future. We had nearly 60 applications for the post and the standard of the applications was very high.

Thank you for your interest in working with us in the role of Administration Assistant. Unfortunately, as you have emailed out of office hours before the deadline, we will not be able to send you an application pack and extend the deadline. Please keep an eye on our website for future opportunities.

We'd like to thank you for your application and for your interest in the role of facilities assistant. The standard of applications has been incredibly high, making this a difficult decision. Unfortunately, on this occasion you have not been shortlisted for interview. Whilst we were impressed with your application, it was felt that your experience did not align with the post as closely as other candidates. We will, however, keep all of your details on record as there may be some upcoming projects in the future which require additional staffing. We wish you every success in the future.

Thank you for your email. Unfortunately, due to the large number of applications that we received we are unable to provide individual feedback on applications. Sorry about this.

Thank you for your application for the role of receptionist at Clydeside Offices. Unfortunately, your application was not shortlisted on this occasion. We had a high number of applications and we regret that we are not able to offer feedback on applications that have not been shortlisted. We would like to thank you for your interest in the project.

Thank you very much for submitting your application for the role of Facilities Assistant at the Scottish Business Alliance. Unfortunately, we were unable to put you forward as a shortlisted candidate for this particular opportunity. We keep your details on file and may contact you concerning other roles. Please let us know if you do not wish to be kept on the database. We suggest you continue to monitor our vacancies and apply for any internships you're interested in. You'll find all our vacancies here or like us on Facebook to receive regular updates direct to your newsfeed.

Thanks so much for your application for the role of Administrator. Apologies for the delay in replying but we have had an overwhelming response to this position and it has taken me longer to get through all the applications. Unfortunately, you haven't been selected for interview in this instance. I thank you for your time and please do keep an eye on our website and Facebook page for further opportunities. We are unable to offer individual feedback on your application at this time.

Pie Kiosk

At the entrance to the stadium people in black shirts gather in clusters between the groups of armed police, mounted police, and staff in hi-vis. That morning you received a text from the agency:

> Good morning all. Just confirming your shift at Hampden Park stadium tomorrow. Please arrive at the stadium for 11.45am. Uniform is long sleeve black shirt, smart black trousers, black socks and black shoes. No jewellery except wedding band and no nail polish or false nails. Men to be clean shaven or neat trimmed beard. Tina will be at Exit 47 to check you in. Please text back to confirm you are ok for your shift tomorrow. Also for your information in light of the terror attacks in Manchester this week please be aware that there will be a heavy police presence and they can stop and ask to carry out a search on you at any time. Please bring as few belongings as possible and try not to bring any bags with you. Any belongings you do bring with you will be put into storage until after your shift. Please do not cancel your shift as for security reasons I am not able to replace you. Please text back to confirm asap thanks Tina.

> Text back, Yes.

The police presence is heavy. They are armed. Their horses are big close up. What use would a horse be if there's an attack? The fans haven't arrived yet. Weaving in and out of the crowd of police officers are more people in black shirts, with black socks, trousers and shoes like yours. Follow them around the wall of the stadium, until they are massed together, queuing between people in high-vis jackets.

Get searched at Exit 47. Sign in with Tina and join the next queue to sign in with the stadium staff. Follow other people in black shirts down breezeblock hallways. There are racks of t-shirts and a table where someone has a list of all the agency staff names. They cross yours off.

Get handed a slip of paper that says your start time but not your finish time. This slip will get signed at the start of your shift and when you leave, to prove you were really there and really did work. This slip allocates you your role: 'Till Worker: Pie Kiosk'

Then queue for the Tennent's t-shirts because the stadium managers don't want you wearing cheap ironed shirts after all. Select a cap from a bin full of caps. Don't wear the first one you pick up because the inner lining is white and smeared with the fake tan of the last person that wore it. Go to Area E and sign in again with the area supervisor. Get your slip signed. Wait for their briefing.

The supervisor tells everyone the running order of the day:

> Bar staff prep drinks before the first half (alcohol allowed), serve drinks. Pie staff sell pies.
> Then, during the first half, everyone tidies up and preps again.
> Half time, bar staff serve drinks (no alcohol), mostly Bovril. Pie staff sell pies.
> Second half, everyone tidies up and preps again (re-stocking the bar fridges etc.).
> After the game the bar will be open for one hour (or longer if there's overtime). There will be no more pies.
> Then you tidy up, re-stock dry snacks and fridges, take out the bins, split your tips, sign out, and go home.

The room is bare, just the bar, kiosk, the staff, and tall round tables for drinks. They will open the main gates soon and let in the crowds. The smell of surface cleaner is replaced by the smell of hops, and sugary cider, then the smell of pies. The bar staff fill plastic cups with pints. Fast as they can, spilling it on their black shoes. The floor will be sticky in minutes. You load the heated kiosk shelves with macaroni pies, steak and ale pies, chicken pies. Stack napkins by the till. Sell them as fast as you can. Always smile. You hear the rumble of voices rising, getting closer. The doors open.

Pet

Dear Stella,
Bob Murray called to cancel his appointment with you tomorrow.

Dear Stella,
I've booked you in the green room to meet James Gillespie tomorrow at 10am.

Dear Stella,
I've ordered a new fern to replace the dead one on your desk.

Dear Stella,
Your neighbour called to say that your dog has bitten his cat. Again.

Dear Stella,
Susanne called to book an appointment with you next Thursday. I've booked her in for 10am, in the yellow room.

Hi Stella,
Your neighbour called again to say your dog got into his garden and tore up his dahlias.

Hi Stella,
Your neighbour called again and says he wants to speak to you directly. He says it is urgent. Please call him on 07790 609 690.

Stella,
Did I ever tell you that I have dogs too? I foster them. I've got nine at the moment.

Hiya,

I am concerned that your neighbour may be prank calling you. He says that the dog is up his apple tree, and that he will hold it hostage there until you turn up and pay the vet bills for his cat. Dogs don't climb trees.

Stella,

It has occurred to me that your neighbour actually put your dog up the tree himself. I have tried calling your landline and mobile. I am currently unable to get hold of you so am going to your home address to resolve this issue with your neighbour myself. I realise it is my duty as your PA to retrieve your dog so that you can focus on work.

Stella!
I have your dog.
I'm keeping him.

Night Mother

Stella:	Is that a script? I can hear you talking to yourself you know.
Bar Tender:	Oh sorry, I didn't see you there. What can I get you?
Stella:	A large Chardonnay please. Is it anything I've heard of? Shakespeare?
Bar Tender:	Coming right up. I'm the daughter in a two-hander about a mother and daughter, and the daughter commits suicide.
Stella:	Sounds cheery. What's it for?
Bar Tender:	A play at the theatre around the corner, near the station.
Stella:	Oh, I know the one.
Bar Tender:	Have you been?
Stella:	Well no, but I know it. I've been to the Kings for the musicals and seen some pantos at the Pavilion.
Bar Tender:	Here you go. Sorry I didn't see you before. We're supposed to greet every customer with a smile. How long were you standing there?
Stella:	Long enough. Don't worry about it. I wouldn't mind that smile though.
Bar Tender:	(smiles and then pretends to frown) Sorry, too late now.
Stella:	(smiles)
Bar Tender:	It's usually quiet during the daytime so I rehearse when no one's around.
Stella:	Don't let me stop you. You said it was a mother daughter thing, right? I can read the mother if you like. I'm probably rubbish but I did drama at school and I loved it. I was Cinderella once.
Bar Tender:	(pauses) Really? That would be helpful actually, thanks. I'm pretty nervous about it. But I should leave you to your drink.

Stella:	Honestly, I could do with the distraction. And the company.
Bar Tender:	Rough day?
Stella:	I'm drinking alone on a Tuesday morning, so yeah, a bit.
Bar Tender:	You want to talk about it?
Stella:	Not really. Shall I hold the script and you do your bit from memory?
Bar Tender:	Well yeah, if you're sure.
Stella:	I'm sure. Where are you from by the way?
Bar Tender:	You mean where are my ancestors from? I was born here.
Stella:	Well when you put it like that, never mind, sorry.
Bar Tender:	That's OK, so the script?
Stella:	Of course.
Bar Tender:	Let's start at the beginning.

Libra

While she's dealing with the cleaners there's the Women's March, the Brexit bill gets passed, and Indyref2 is rejected by Westminster. There's a fire in Glasgow and a mudslide in Sierra Leone, and Grenfell, Charlottesville, Trump's latest Tweets, and Guam, and Las Ramblas, and all these things are on low volume above the sofas that no one is sitting on in the waiting room area where people sometimes sit and sip water from a glass that feels strange because it has been in the dishwasher recently. These people, when they do come in, sign their names in the visitor's book, and then sign out again when they leave. But mostly no one sits on the sofa, and the receptionist is alone behind a desk that has nothing personal on it because of the clear desk policy. She put up post-its around her laptop for a while, but these were deemed a security hazard, as the cleaners might read them, and then the confidential information would not be confidential anymore, and she would be in trouble for causing a security breach and maybe get fired but probably just have a disciplinary.

And so she emails the cleaners about why they don't empty the dishwashers in the morning even though she keeps leaving them comments in the cleaner communication folder, about how they should be emptying the dishwasher. The reason she is emailing them instead of leaving another comment in the communications folder, is that someone from accounts emailed her, complaining that the dishwashers were always full of clean dishes in the morning. This was a problem because then when the people in accounts ate their breakfast, they put the dirty bowls in on top of the clean ones, and then they weren't clean anymore.

Good afternoon all,

I've been advised that people are putting dirty breakfast bowls in the dishwashers with the clean crockery. I am in ongoing discussions with the cleaners about why they don't empty these dishwashers.

Until they start doing so, please check that you're not mixing the clean and dirty crockery as it means that the clean things have to be washed again.

I've also been advised that the weighing scales in the 6th floor disabled bathroom have disappeared. If anyone knows where they are please let me know.

I'm not 100% sure if the person who took the scales was from our office, or the one on the floor above. They have been known to use our bathrooms. However yesterday I saw a middle-aged man in a suit that I've not seen before leaving down the stairs and he came from the righthand side as if from the gent's toilets. Didn't see any of our lanyards so it probably wasn't someone from our office. If anyone sees this man, please let me know.

Also, this is to let you know that the toilet paper dispenser in the 3rd cubicle of the 6th floor women's bathroom is broken and keeps falling open. I am arranging for this to be fixed asap. Have a lovely day!

Kind regards,

Astrid

The cleaning issues continue through the spring and summer and there are attacks in Westminster, Manchester, on London Bridge, in Borough Market, and in Finsbury Park, on low volume. The signing-in sheets fill the reception folder and Astrid orders more ring binders, starts another sign-in folder. Anthony Joshua wins. The Conservative Party sign a deal with the DUP. She orders an ergonomic chair assessment for one of the women in HR who has back problems. She does not get permission to order the ergonomic chair the woman requested. The agency tells her that she will no longer be needed from next week, as the woman whose job she's covering will be returning from maternity leave. During her last week, on the day of the Parson's Green attack in September, two good things happen.

Good afternoon all,

This is to let you know that the toilet paper dispenser in the 3rd cubicle of the 6th floor women's bathroom has been fixed.

I've been advised that people are continuing to put dirty breakfast bowls in the dishwashers with the clean crockery. I am still in ongoing discussions with the cleaners about why they don't empty these dishwashers. Until they start doing so, please check that you're not mixing the clean and dirty crockery as it means that the clean things have to be washed again.

I've also been advised that the weighing scales in the 6th floor disabled bathroom have been found in the bathroom they disappeared from. If anyone knows who borrowed them, please let me know. In any case, I'm sure we're all glad to have them back!

Kind regards,

Astrid

Empty Boxes

They were working a Saturday night shift at the bar and taking out the empty boxes when Duncan told Inga about the glade. He said her hair reminded him of the autumn leaves that gathered at the bottom there, beneath the little ledge. There were no leaves by the bins. Just bits of plastic that drifted along the concrete. He climbed onto the stack of cardboard in the giant bin and jumped on it, to flatten the boxes, make room for more. He told her about the oak tree in this glade, really old and beautiful, good for climbing. He had built a rope swing there once with his little sister. In autumn they would swing off the ledge, let go and fall into a pile of leaves. The swinging sometimes shook down more, and he would lie there in a storm of gold. He asked if he'd ever told her about Danae and the shower of gold.

It started with a beautiful woman, he said, with red hair.

The Greeks never had red hair, she said. Besides, I dye mine. It's mouse brown really, or dishwater blonde.

Fine, he said. Danae was a beautiful woman with hair the colour of a mouse in dishwater, and she was walking in a beautiful glade when she paused to rest against an oak tree.

Do you think there are oak trees in Greece? Inga said.

Fine, he said. I won't tell you. It's a nasty story anyway. You can come see the glade for yourself when you visit. My Ma keeps asking when she's going to meet you.

He climbed out of the bin and peeled gaffer tape off the bottom of his shoe.

When Inga arrived at his mother's flat two weeks later Duncan wasn't there. She had planned to surprise him. Instead she was having a cup of tea with Deirdre, his mother, who had no idea where he was. She didn't ask Deirdre if she knew about what happened with the university. Instead, sitting next to each other on a floral sofa, Inga asked her where the rope swing glade was.

Inga walked along the path and turned right at the fallen tree, following a little trail through the curling ferns, moss beneath her sandals. There were mushroom fairy rings in loops and the green light spilled through the leaves. The light was never natural at work. They had dim yellow bulbs and candles. The area by the bins was always floodlit. Coming home at dawn, the sky was that weak kind of blue with the streetlamps still on and the shop displays illuminated for no-one to see. She'd lie in bed and fall asleep as the curtains leaked the afternoon into her room. Thin, flower-patterned curtains that came with the flat.

Here there were real flowers, bluebells, empty bottles of Buckfast, and little white flowers she didn't know the name of. She nearly walked off the ledge when she reached it. It wasn't very high, and the bottom was green and brown, with moss, ferns, and more little mushrooms. She wondered if they were edible. They looked different from those perfect, round white ones at Tesco, or the half-moons they served in the stroganoff special at work, floating in cream. In France they'd set up an aisle for the ugly fruit and veg that normally got rejected by supermarkets, the stuff that was usually thrown away. They sold it cheap. Apparently it was popular. Lumpy apples, bent cucumbers, that sort of thing. Did Duncan know about that? He would like it, she thought.

She couldn't see the rope swing. Maybe this was the wrong place. It was the wrong colour. But then, there was that big, beautiful oak on her left. The branches rustled overhead, thick with leaves. Birds perhaps. What would they have here, wood pigeons? She sat on the ledge and kicked her feet backwards and forwards just above the ground.

Deirdre had shown Inga his room as if she'd asked. There were shelves with all the books he'd left behind. The Harry Potter series, some teenage fantasy novels, comic books. She'd never heard of *Oor Wullie* till she moved to Glasgow. She had asked him once about his favourite childhood stories. How like him to lie about something so pointless. To say instead that he'd read children's versions of the Greek myths. Duncan had laughed when she told him she liked

Oor Wullie and said he'd never read them himself. Just like he said he'd never read that article about Ovid, so he couldn't possibly have known that he was plagiarising it. He couldn't steal someone else's words if he didn't know they'd been used before, could he? Great minds think alike, right?

Yes. And what else?

He used Jupiter and Zeus interchangeably in his essays. He paraphrased inaccurately and went pages over the word count. They failed him twice and then the thing with the Ovid essay happened. Instead of telling her about it straightaway he'd told her, by the bins, the story of the laurel tree.

Daphne is a beautiful nymph, he had said. She has red hair, dyed. She's tee-total and a bit frigid.

Thanks, Inga said. Subtle.

And Apollo is so inflamed with desire he takes her hand, he said.

He took Inga's hand.

He kneels, Duncan said.

He knelt.

And he begs her to be his lover.

Duncan winked. Inga shook her head, raised an eyebrow.

Fine, that bit was sleazy, he said. Daphne has every right to fuck off and she does.

He stood up but kept hold of Inga's fingers.

She frolics off into the wood and he, being a sleaze, pursues her. He asks her over and over and the faster she runs the faster he has to run to keep up, to be heard. She disappears amongst the trees in a wood. He stops hearing her footsteps. He's like, where are you Daphs?

Inga pulled her fingers away and held her hand over a pretend yawn.

The manager rapped his knuckles on the bar. Oi, he said. Time to lean time to clean, people. They both nodded and opened the glass washer, started polishing with wet towels.

And lo and behold, Duncan whispered, she's turned into a tree. He digs her out of the ground and plants her in his garden. Keeps her forever. Uses the bay leaves in his cooking. What do you think of that?

Jared walked in, still tying on his apron. Late again.

Mate, he said. Is it true about what happened?

Duncan laughed. The day they kicked Duncan out of university he laughed all evening. He'd never got so many tips, £80 in twenties.

Fuck 'em, Jared said, pouring out glasses of champagne for the event. Fuck 'em all, who needs a pompous bit of paper written in Latin anyway?

After they closed it was drinks all around. At 4am they raised their glasses to the University of Life. Duncan did impressions of his professors, put a mop on his head, and minced across the room waving a bottle around.

Now who wants another shot of ivory tower bullshit? he said.

Jared raised his hand and jumped up.

Sir, he said, me sir!

Duncan held the bottle over Jared's open mouth and poured until he choked. Then he did the same to himself and finished it. The night bus driver wouldn't let him on because he was too drunk. They walked over the bridge together and stayed at her flat. He complimented her on the floral curtains and said they reminded him of his mother's sofa.

When Inga woke up it was still dark outside. Duncan was standing at the window, forehead pressed against the glass. He trembled with cold and whisky. His breath formed white drops of condensation in streetlamp light. She sat up. He kept staring out.

I can't go back to uni, he said. How can I tell them? I'm the only one in my family to get in and I can't go back.

Inga went to the university and spent her lunch break alone, eating peanut butter and jam sandwiches in the library. They had had nearly a year of sitting in the canteen complaining about the food and saying they would start bringing in packed lunches. Nearly a year of Classics for him. For her it was Cognitive Approaches to Mind and Behaviour, Biological Approaches to Mind and Behaviour, Life-Span Psychology, History and Theory of Psychology, Research Design and Analysis, Statistical Analysis. She drew foxes and pigeons in the margins of her notes. She coloured in her map of the human brain. She drew neurons and synapses with little faces and speech bubbles: *I'm part of a thought!*

Nearly a year of doing fortnightly experiments and writing up reports on response rates to images, to emotive words, to number sequences. Every report they broke down with t-tests, with the median, the mode, or the mean. They tried to find causality and got correlations instead. Every paper she got back had *well done* written next to it. Then she went to work and heard stories about people transforming into trees and birds. Stories of men fighting rivers and Juno putting the hundred eyes of her dead monster into the tail of her peacock. Of Orpheus journeying to the underworld. And now she was eating sandwiches alone in the library.

Before they kicked him out, Duncan had taken that woman with the clarinet and tried to make her Orpheus too, but Inga wouldn't let him. Walking home at 4am she had seen a window full of yellow light. The walls were blue and a woman in pyjamas was facing her, playing a clarinet. Inga could see her glance down at her music sheets and then watch her reflection. She didn't look beyond the glass, didn't see Inga pause on her walk home. Inga crossed the street and stood under the window, so she could hear better. It was *Rhapsody in Blue*, or parts of it. The woman kept going over the same bits again and again. Even though the window was closed the clarinet was loud, piercing.

One of the windows opposite banged open and a man put both hands on the sill and stuck his head out, yelling, SHUT UP. The music faltered, then carried on.

Shut up shutup shutupshutup, he yelled, then banged the window shut again.

She kept playing.

Inga stayed under the window until the roar of the bin men's truck drowned the music out. After her next shift, she tried to find the same house again, but all the windows in the street were dark. Maybe the clarinet woman had had an exam coming up and that's why she'd stayed up all night. Or a performance. Or maybe she was feeling something strong that she didn't feel anymore. Either way, all the houses looked the same in the dawn light.

After her next shift, Inga told Duncan about it while they were eating the leftover canapés at work.

What do you think? she said.

Well, he said. Have I told you about Orpheus?

Oh, here we go, said Jared, getting up. I'm off for a smoke.

No, you haven't, she said. Is he another god pursuing some nymph? What's that got to do with the clarinet?

Well, he said. You'll like this one. He pinned two salmon and cucumber mini sandwiches onto a toothpick, then added a lump of blue cheese. Orpheus, he said, goes to the underworld to beg for his wife back. She died obviously. He sings, playing this tune on his lyre which is so beautiful that Hades cries and says he can have her back. Maybe your flute lady…

Clarinet, I think, Inga said, picking up another olive tapenade crostini.

Whatever, he said, putting the toothpick stacked pink, green and blue into his mouth, then pulling it out clean. Maybe she's playing an ode to call her lover back.

So, Orpheus and his wife, they live happily ever after? Inga said. She could feel the tapenade stuck between her two front teeth. That's not how your stories usually go.

Don't blame me, blame the Romans, he said. Or the Greeks. He waved a cocktail sausage in the air and then ate it. And no, of course that's not how it ends. He gets her back on the condition that he doesn't look at her till they're safe and what does he do? How could he resist? Duncan took three more sausages and stuffed them into his mouth.

He could resist if he really wanted her back, she said.

Well maybe he didn't want her that badly. Maybe he was just seeing what he could get away with. Seeing how powerful his music was, how persuasive.

She had left Deidre after half an hour of waiting for him to turn up. He would probably say that it was a misunderstanding, that she shouldn't have expected him to be in. But it was not the first time he had stood her up. She would say something this time. Although he had been good to her, mostly, she would not agree to meet up with him outside work again. Although the sink had got blocked on her first day at work and she'd emptied all the half-drunk bottles into it before she realised. Although she then smashed two champagne glasses and was worried she wouldn't get to keep the job, was worried Duncan would get in trouble for having recommended her to the boss. Although Duncan had taken a cork and floated it on the wine dark sea in the sink, and said don't worry Penelope, I'm here. She would say no.

During her shift the next day, the bar filled up with people in Gore-Tex and hiking boots. They were talking and laughing loudly in another language. Dutch, she guessed, from the throaty sounds they used, from the accents of the ones talking to Jared in English, asking him for pints of the most Scottish beer available. Someone peeled off their socks and hung them on the grate where they stiffened and smoked. Inga could hear the new waitress Pandora talking to the chef about how hungover she was, and how many shots she'd had the night before at Sub Club, and how Duncan had probably had twice as many. Duncan was telling the manager Massimo that he was late because of flooding on the railway line.

One of the tourists, a man with a white beard, overheard Duncan and asked Inga if it flooded often. He asked if she knew about the 1953 North Sea Flood. She did not.

Half of Holland was underwater, the man with the white beard said. Oh yes, he smiled, looking at a spot a little ahead of him where he could see the debris floating. It was terrible. People were climbing on top of their roofs and filling their prams with antiques.

So he'd been out at Sub Club with Pandora. Inga frowned at the man with the white beard, who didn't notice, and continued talking. And if she challenged Duncan about it, what could she say? He hadn't promised her anything. And if he thought she was upset, which of his characters would he wheel out? Diana, who ordered Acteon's own hounds to tear him to pieces because he glimpsed her bathing naked. Salamacis who'd stalked Hermaphroditus and clung to him so fiercely that they became one body. Echo, who repeated Narcissus' own words back to him until she faded into nothingness, just a voice, repeating whatever he said.

There were cows floating upside down, the man with the beard said. With their legs in the air, straight like this. He stuck his arms out straight in front of him. Can you believe it?

The next time they arranged to meet, Duncan suggested the beach at Troon. He was not there when she arrived. The sky was white. The grass at his feet was bent from the wind and seemed to lean away from him. On the other side of the road the grass gave way to rocks and a thin strip of grey sand. Inga was there, crouched at the edge of the foam. It curled around and over her feet. He couldn't see what she was holding. Perhaps a mermaid's purse had washed up with the seaweed and plastic bags. When Duncan was a child, he'd collected mermaid's purses and dead crabs and lined them up on his windowsill. At night, the smell made him feel like he was at the bottom of the sea. He imagined himself inside a lobster pot, watching the green world around him, the yellow beams of light reaching down from above. He liked those sea dreams, though in the morning the bed was always wet.

She was poking in the sand. She paused; hand placed on something firm. Maybe it was a message in a bottle. How many messages had he and his little sister sent out? Their home phone number was still the same, but no one had called. Some bottles were bound to come back to the beach, he supposed, if they hadn't been thrown out far enough. But no. It was a black wellington boot. She turned away from the waves and held it upside down. He watched her empty it onto the sand and pick the little bits up, moving them around, arranging them. Her hair hung down over her face. Her crouched figure broke the line of foam that lapped at the sand.

Duncan used to sail a little plastic boat in the nearby rock pools with his little sister. The Uselyss had navigated between the siren limpets, had avoided the anemone Scylla and the crab with lopsided claws, Crabdis. His sister, crouched with bare feet in the sand, splashed the water and tried to capsize the boat but lo! (whenever the ship survived another obstacle Duncan shouted lo!), the Uselyss emerged unscathed, shiny, plastic, and blue. And there, on the other side of the pool, waiting in a dress made from the finger of a rubber glove, was his beautiful wife, the clothes peg, Penelope. It was one of those clothes pegs that was old fashioned and wooden with a round ball on the top. They had drawn a smiley face on it. He wondered what had happened to Penelope and the little ship.

But Inga had found only the sea, not the tiny ocean. She held the boot in both hands and turned it over. Out poured pebbles, sea-smoothed glass, broken shells and a ring pull. She wiped grains of sand on her trousers. There were always the things you expect to see, which no one looks at. That's what she was looking for. Like the things she found during her late shifts. Broken glass on wet sofas. The stem of a champagne flute. Half-eaten fish cakes on the tables, ribbons and cake on the floor. A single earring shaped like a star. She'd picked up the earring, the stem of a champagne flute, the ribbon, and lined them up on her windowsill. When the peel dried it lost its colour, but the smell was good. Perhaps she would do something with these pieces. The ring pull, the sea smoothed glass, the shell with a hole in the middle. That pebble, yellow and wet. And the boot? Whose boot had it been? The number 10 was raised and worn in rubber on the bottom. Was Duncan a size 10? She had no idea.

And where was he now? He had said he might take her for a boat ride but she couldn't see any boats nearby. Perhaps it was a joke. But then, what if he had rented a boat from somewhere and already gone out in it? She could hear him preparing the story before he'd even stepped on board. How he was an adventurer on the wine dark sea. He had said that to her once, about how someone or other had crossed the wine dark sea. The billowing silk sea.

She could see a seal's head out in the bay, not far from her. The sun shone on its oily skin. Its nostrils flared, and she heard a snorting, huffing sound. It ducked out of sight then rose again, a little closer, its whiskers hung with silver beads. She trailed her fingers in the foam. She looked up at the gulls wheeling, white, above them. She held up a piece of glass, rubbed her thumb across the smooth surface. It was made from sand and now here it was, returned to where it came from. What do you think about that, seal? She held up the piece of glass. The seal looked at her and snuffed. Beads of water dripped from its whiskers. She shook her head and stood up. She left the boot on the beach and turned towards Duncan. She saw him and waved. The boot broke the line where the waves met the sand.

Dragonflies

It took her days to finish watching *Amélie*. Not because it was a long film, but because as soon as the little girl had raspberries lined up on her fingertips and started to eat them in fast forward, Connie fell asleep. She was always waking up in the cinema to the sound of fold-down chairs snapping back into place as people pulled their coats on. If they were crying, she knew she'd missed a good film. If they were laughing and talking in their little twos and threes, then it was guaranteed. Mostly, they left silently, with the blank expressions of people who have been staring at a screen for two hours. Those faces didn't tell her anything about the film she'd just sat through, and then she really wished she'd been awake.

The cinema ran old, foreign, and arthouse films. She sold ice cream and popcorn, crisps made of chickpeas, wine, bottled soft drinks, tea and coffees, and keep-cups with the cinema name written across them. She could watch what she wanted, when she wanted, whilst eating as much popcorn as possible. She could re-arrange her shifts whenever she had an audition.

How many times had she been humming along to 'Sweet Transvestite', during their Halloween season, only to wake up with crumbs stuck to her chest? Or watched the set up to a thriller only to miss the twist? Or seen John Travolta and Samuel L. Jackson swaggering about to her favourite soundtrack, only to cut to the bit in the credits where they told you that no animals had been harmed in the making of the film? Were there even animals in Pulp Fiction? What about the scenes where the characters were eating meat, if that ever happened, what then? Did they have to make sure the chickens died before shooting began?

She liked to pick out funny names in the credits and had made a note of Big Mac, Erik Porn, Oswald Gummidge and Yolanda Squatpump. Her name would be up there eventually. She liked it when films 'based on a true story' had the get out clause at the end where they said that: *All characters appearing in this work are fictitious.*

Any resemblance to real persons, living or dead, is purely coincidental. She liked knowing the theme music without having listened to the full soundtrack. Often, back at home, she'd watch the trailer for the film she'd just sat through, so she knew all the best bits and could repeat the jokes if conversation ever called for it. Conversation never did. Conversation usually turned to her auditions, if she had any, and what they were like, and if she thought she would get the role.

Some of her favourite openings were *The Big Lebowski, O Brother, Where Art Thou?* and, when they showed old kid's films on Tuesday afternoons, *The Lion King* (the original version). Everything after those openings blurred and the pixels seemed to grow large and out of focus. Just colours moving about in front of her and the hum of the music and characters talking. Sometimes she would remember the hum of red and blue dragonflies darting over the pond at home. And then she woke up and shook popcorn from her clothes.

Bright blue and red the insects hummed over the dark surface of the pond. Here landing on a string of duckweed, there on the water, only to lift up again. Sometimes they flew together, the red one underneath, the blue above.

She kicked off her sandals and lay on the warm patio. The tiles smelled of dirt. She watched, from under the brim of her sun cap, the dragonflies flicker and drone. She pretended the red one had burnt in the shimmer of heat that summer, and that the blue one was flying over it to protect it. But that was silly. Only people burnt. The cap was to cover her peeling nose, slick with sun cream. The cap had a dolphin on it, from when they went to Florida last year. She had burnt then too. But the dragonflies didn't need sun cream. They were eggs first, safe in the water, then larvae, nymphs swimming about with sharp pincers. Then up they shimmered, trembling over the surface. Always new, always becoming something else. Her skin would peel.

She would be someone else. She would be cast in a play, perhaps by Chekhov, and become one of the three sisters. Or an arthouse film, ideally a period drama about a woman writer trying to break out of the shadow of her husband's work. Something that could get her critical recognition. Or maybe an advert that would get her enough money to live on for a year, and do as much unpaid theatre as she liked, or maybe voiceover work, or probably the role of a supportive girlfriend on a sitcom about a young man coming of age. She'd had several auditions lately. She'd get a call back soon.

Ending:

Connie left the cinema crying.

Alternative ending:

Connie left the cinema laughing and talking with friends.

Alternative ending:

Connie woke up.

Alternative ending:

Connie got a call back.

Alternative ending:

Connie left the cinema with the blank expression of someone who has just been staring at a screen for two hours.

Credits:

Connie McCleod

[...]

No animals were harmed in the making of this film.

[...]

All characters appearing in this work are fictitious. Any resemblance to real persons, living or dead, is purely coincidental.

Disciplinary

Massimo had never had a disciplinary before. He had been in the industry ten years without receiving any official complaints. Yes, he was friendly, perhaps over friendly. But he was more like a mate than a boss really. Yes, his approach could be considered unconventional. It could also be considered fun.

And Jared had always given as good as he got. He laughed at Massimo's risqué jokes. He returned every pinch, slap, squeeze. He laughed when he batted Massimo away or told him – you can't say that. And Massimo treated his male and female staff just the same. None of the women had ever complained. They laughed and pinched and squeezed too.

Jared had dropped out of university and worked full time at the bar now. He'd been there for three years, longer than anyone else, and had never had a promotion. He got good tips and did a lot of double shifts. He always had a pen behind each ear, and one in his black ponytail. Often, when they were busy, he went without a break, even though some of the newer staff demanded theirs. The ones that reminded Massimo about their right to a break never lasted long.

Jared spent a lot of time when it was quiet smoking by the bins and talking to the chefs about the difficult customers. The chefs were always sneaking him chips and telling him he was too skinny. He spent a lot of time living on people's sofas after his boyfriend left him for a blues guitarist and kicked him out. Now, he was staying in the sous chef's spare room while she looked for a paying lodger.

Everyone knew about the disciplinary. The other waiters said they felt sorry for Jared, when they talked to him about it. They said it was outrageous that Massimo had been able to get away with it for so long. He'd definitely gone too far this time. Pushed him up against a wall and –

They said that Jared had done the right thing reporting him. When Jared asked if they wanted to come forward with their own stories, they told him they'd love to but – and then they'd rush off to check on their tables.

They said, when Massimo asked them, that he didn't make them feel uncomfortable, they could take a joke. When he asked them to come forward with character testaments for him, they said they would love to, but they didn't want to get involved and were really busy, and – they rushed off to check their tables.

When they were out of earshot the other waiters said to each other that of course it was brave of Jared and argued about whether Massimo was really that bad. Everyone knew someone who knew someone that had been fired for making complaints at one restaurant or another. Everyone had put Jared up at some point. Everyone had been pinched, slapped, squeezed by Massimo.

After the disciplinary, Massimo waited a few months before offering Jared the role of supervisor. In those three months he had mostly observed the boundaries that had been laid out in the disciplinary. He had, mostly, kept his hands to himself.

Well, he asked Jared, what do you think? The role comes with a pay rise.

It was the end of a late shift and the waiters were wiping down tables when Massimo pulled him aside and offered him the promotion. The other waiters, who had been talking as they worked, went silent. Jared looked at him strangely and put down his cloth. He took a pen out from behind his ear and put it back again.

Lakeside Café

He sits there every day, has done all summer. We named him Lemon Iced Tea. Every time he pays for one, I can see the edge of a tattoo on his wrist. It peeks in swirls from under his shirt sleeve. As we pretend to clean the coffee machine, we try to guess what the rest of the tattoo is. He sits at the table right by the lake railing and throws crumbs to the ducks. It peeks in swirls.

Nina says it's some Indian symbol or script. And look, she says, at the cuff of the other sleeve, a frayed bracelet of coloured string. Like the friendship bracelets we used to make when we were little.

You'd have to wear it even when the colours faded into dirt. You couldn't take it off to wash it because if you cut it, you'd break the bond. But somehow, I don't have mine anymore. I don't remember cutting it off. Perhaps it frayed, loosened, broke.

Or the bracelet could be from Paris, I say. Remember those men all around Montmartre? Who come up and start talking to you, binding these things tight onto your wrist, free of charge, free of charge. Then when it's on, they ask for a donation. Remember? Maybe it's one of those, I say. Maybe he didn't know how to say no to the bracelet men. He probably gave them a euro and everything.

No, she says. He would have cut it off if it meant nothing. She walks to the sink and her anklet jingles.

He's a bit old for friendship bracelets, I said. And a bit, you know, male.

He doesn't think like that, she says. When you travel, you make friends for life all over the world, which you might never see again.

Not exactly friends for life then, are they? I say.

Don't be like that. You know what I mean, she says. And some you do see.

She walks back towards me. The bells jingle, brush against her ankle, against a string of thread, colours faded, dirty.

The Sting

Davey Smiles had not been invited to the staff meeting. Everyone else in the hotel kitchen was invited, all the chefs – Ewelina, Hamid, Mo, Hassan, Paulo and probably Cameron, though Davey hadn't spoken to him about it yet. Even Magda, the other kitchen porter, was going to be there. The manager was updating the system, and needed to verify everyone's documents again. Did that mean they didn't want Davey's details? Did that mean they didn't want him anymore? Was he fired? It was the thing about the stock take not adding up, things missing, that got him thinking he'd done something wrong. He was walking along the Clyde, which always helped him to think.

But Massimo had promised him, at his interview, that his record would never be a problem. We don't discriminate here, he said. What you've done in the past is the past. Everybody has been in trouble with the police, at one point or another, and if they haven't, they haven't lived, right? That's what Massimo said, the day Davey was hired. Davey didn't ask, back then, what Massimo had got in trouble for. It didn't seem appropriate, for a job interview.

Since then, of course, they'd spent many nights raiding the hotel bar, trying to outdrink each other. They woke up once, Massimo on the floor of the beer cellar, Davey sprawled across the kegs. They'd never been so cold. Best manager he'd ever had. They compared stories of drunken nights out, one-night stands, the time Davey lost half his front teeth, the night he lost the other half, the stag do where Massimo smuggled cocaine through customs. They competed scandal for scandal. Davey usually won, but not always. He could do a good impression of Massimo, whose hair was too long, with a mop. He'd never seen anyone slap their thighs laughing, but Massimo did.

Massimo never minded if he was a bit late for work, as long as he finished on time. It's only washing dishes anyway, he said. Nope, the manager didn't mind when the occasional bit of food or bottle of Buckfast went missing. Or when the stock sheets were off, and Ewelina was raging around, pointing her finger at him. Massimo said they overcharged people so much that it didn't matter. Once you got people drunk you could add anything you wanted to their tab, and they'd never notice. Ewelina disagreed. Everything mattered, she said, and she could not do her job properly if stock was missing. And she always knew to point the finger in his direction when he was suds-deep to his elbows in the sink and couldn't protest without bubbles going everywhere, making him look ridiculous.

Once, she went too far and shouted at Massimo – *Curva*, why do you let him steal? You know this man is a criminal.

Davey couldn't hear himself shouting because Massimo was louder, and all in Italian, and they couldn't understand a word he was saying. Finally Massimo said, quietly, in English: Everybody is a criminal, and no one is guilty, ok? Ok. Do not swear at me again.

After that, nothing went missing for a while. Then, when it did, no one said anything about it.

But maybe Massimo had been biding his time since then, looking for an excuse to get rid of him, tired of his stories and his talent for making things disappear. Or perhaps he had decided that one of them had to go, and of course, between a chef or a kitchen porter, who was more disposable? It wasn't even a question. It was Davey's day off and they were all in this meeting without him.

He walked along the Clyde, watching the gulls and cranes dip and swing, the clouds scudding in the wind. Why did he keep taking things when he knew? He knew he'd get in trouble again eventually. But then, it was Massimo's fault really, for saying that it didn't matter when it did. Massimo had encouraged him, if truth be told, to take whatever he wanted. And he'd defended Davey when he did just that.

Ah, but he couldn't really blame Massimo, could he? The law was the law, and Davey knew it well. He was to blame. He took what was not his. He did it knowingly and that was the problem. He was addicted to making things disappear from the hotel kitchen and reappear in his own fridge. And yet, other addictions went unpunished. (Here he thought he saw a fish swimming upstream – surely the Clyde was too dirty for salmon?) There were alcoholics in the hotel bar, drinking for hours every night. They were always telling the bar staff – Duncan mostly, he liked stories – the same things over and over again. Massimo did impersonations of them. Not as good as Davey's, but they were funny anyway. There was Tottenham Joe, from England, who sang football songs, and undid a button of his shirt after each pint. There was Tony, the former jockey who could name every horse he'd ever ridden, and how fast each one was, and where they came in each race. He was shorter than Davey, that jockey, which made a nice change. There was Daryl the Barrel, Wee Mickey, Ginger, Sneaky Pete, and the old man with the funny bow ties.

There was Stella, who was very successful apparently, and always bought mineral water for her little dog. Last night, the big story was that the dog had been stolen. Stella was on her second bottle of pinot grigio when she started crying. Her PA, she cried, whom she had trusted all those years to take care of her, had stolen her little dog. Her little Prince, her Bobby. She slammed her hand on the bar and Duncan, who was leaning towards her sympathetically, flinched. Pandora, the new waitress, rolled her eyes at Davey.

What kind of psycho, Stella said, steals a helpless wee dog from his mammy?

Duncan shook his head, trying not to smile. Davey did not feel like smiling. Did stealing make you a psycho? He was perfectly sane. More sane than Stella, at any rate, who kept slapping the bar and crying, and drinking wine, the bottle of mineral water, unopened, on the bar in front of her. It was that incident, with the dog and Stella crying, and then the stock take where lots of stuff turned out to be missing, that got him so worried about not being invited to the team meeting. Otherwise he would've seen it coming, the real reason behind the whole thing. But it wasn't until Cameron messaged him and asked if he wanted to go to the pub, that he realised he'd been following the wrong line of thought the whole time.

Cameron's message read: your day off 2 yeah? Bored. Beer?

Well, Davey wasn't one to drink before midday, but he said yes, because he wanted to know why Cameron wasn't at the meeting. He wanted to ask, face to face, what was going on. (He saw two more fish leaping upstream, and began walking quickly, trying to keep pace with them. Where had they come from? Were there more?) Because at that moment his thoughts went in a new direction, like a train that was shunted onto a different track. Cameron was the head chef, and he was good, no way would anyone fire him. He drank early, yes, but not too much. He was never late, and his cooking was stellar (Stella – would she ever get her dog back? Was her PA a psycho? Was he? Were either of them guilty, even if they were criminals? That was the most memorable sentence Massimo had ever said to him, and he'd thought about it a lot). Cameron wasn't getting fired and nor was he. Cameron would know what was going on.

He and Cameron didn't have much in common besides work. Cameron talked football to anyone who'd listen and anyone who wouldn't. He talked socialist politics the rest of the time. Davey didn't like football or politics much. Football was boring and politics was depressing. Wars wars wars. Cuts cuts cuts. Votes votes votes. Blah blah blah.

But he'd never say that to Cameron, because Cameron would go on about socialism, and communism, and Scottish Labour, and Davey would be bored out of his mind. No. There was one obvious thing that Davey had in common with Cameron, and that none of the others had. They were both Scottish. Cameron was born in Paisley, and Davey was born in Dalmuir. They'd lived in the country their whole lives. Been on holiday plenty of times, sure, but always lived here. Davey had been to Europe a few times, and even went to Cancun once, a long time ago. And Cameron used to go to Greece every year when he had a Greek girlfriend, and now went to Karachi every year with his Pakistani girlfriend.

So, Davey thought (watching the fish, which were definitely salmon, swimming up the Clyde) where did everyone in the team meeting come from? He wasn't even sure, really. He guessed most were from Europe. It was probably just some admin. Maybe an assurance that Brexit wouldn't affect their rights. Yes, that'd be it. Brexit. Cameron would probably know the details. Being head chef, he knew things management wouldn't tell everybody. Davey paused (he had lost sight of the fish) and watched the gulls dipping over the river. He messaged Cameron, saying he'd meet him at the Clutha for a pint.

Yes, Cameron would definitely know. But he'd probably want to talk about the 'I' word. Immigration. That was the big thing they disagreed on. Cameron said one thing, he said another. It was or wasn't good for the economy. It should or shouldn't be capped, or more tightly regulated. Davey tapped his phone against his teeth. He had nothing against foreigners, but there were only so many jobs, he thought. And only the other week they had a new cleaner, Deirdre, who'd lost her previous job at the check-out to a machine. It would be everyone vs machines eventually, but for now it was just people like them that were losing out. Competing against foreigners (he had nothing against them) and machines (he had lots against them) was not bound to be good for anyone except the machines. His opinions were his. Call it realistic, he thought, or call it xenophobic, as Cameron often did. Each to their own opinion. But then, he wasn't in competition with any of his colleagues. Even Magda, the other kitchen porter, wasn't his competitor. They did the same job on different days, that was all.

Davey tapped his phone against his teeth. (A gull dropped to the surface of the river and snatched at something – the salmon? – and missed, coming back up with nothing). Well, and where were they from then? He knew where Magda and Ewelina were from, and Hamid. But what about Hassan and Mo? He had no idea. And anyway, it was probably just paperwork. Massimo was Italian, and he was on their side. He defended people when they were put in a tight spot, even if they were in the wrong. He'd said it himself: everyone was a criminal, but nobody was guilty. He was probably helping them out right now.

Davey Smiles carried on along the riverbank until he saw Cameron on the other side of the traffic lights just outside the Clutha, waving. Cameron strode across the road towards him and said – Davey, did you know there was a staff meeting today and we weren't invited?

Daffodils

Stella: I'll drink too much while we go through your script, become embarrassed, cry, leave.

Bar Tender: I'll invite you to my play as you put your coat on.

Stella: I'll come.

Bar Tender: You'll come.

Stella: It's a small theatre. You're wearing your own clothes because there's no budget for costumes.

Bar Tender: I see you in the back row, the programme crushed tight in your hands, watching me.

Stella: After you see me your voice gets louder, your highs higher, your lows lower. It's almost too much but not too much. But maybe your voice doesn't change at all.

Bar Tender: Some of my friends are in the audience. I invite you out for drinks with us afterwards.

Stella: I don't know anyone. I don't know what to say.

Bar Tender: You thrust some crumpled daffodils into my hands and leave.

Stella: You come after me, you ask me to stay.

Bar Tender: You say yes, you will, yes, and you stay.

Bulldog

Hassan and Mo were gone. There was a short piece in the local newspaper about it. Some students gathered outside the building, waving placards shouting and singing songs. Davey read that a couple of them had tried to prevent the deportation flight but were stopped by security and arrested. Now they were in the news. The rest of the students stopped turning up. They were probably protesting the arrests.

Massimo hired two new chefs, one from Edinburgh, the other from England. The English one, Daisy, used to be an army chef. She kept a close eye on the stock. When he spoke, she often squinted, like she didn't understand his accent, but he wasn't sure. She saw Davey looking at her British bulldog tattoo on her first day and rolled up her sleeve so he could see it properly. Told him she'd got it when she joined up. Didn't hurt at all. Quite expensive though. She'd left London because it was so expensive. The only thing she missed was football, she was an Arsenal fan. Now she'd have to find a Scottish team to support. She asked if he supported Celtic or Rangers. He told her he didn't follow football. He preferred cricket. He liked to listen to the radio while he worked, and the cricket commentary was soothing, rhythmical. He told her which neighbourhoods would take against her tattoo and told her about where it was safe to wear Celtic green, where it was safe to wear Rangers blue. The tattoo was on her forearm in thick black ink. Her skin was covered in burns, but you could still clearly see the shape of the dog's face, the grinning teeth, the cigar and spiked collar.

When Davey told her about Hassan and Mo, she shook her head. It wasn't right to do it in that underhand way, saying there was a staff meeting, she said. But, she shrugged, if you're going to come illegally what do you expect? The law is the law. If you're going to move here you have to do it the right way just like everybody else. He wasn't sure about that, but he didn't like to get into politics. Besides, she was easy to work with, efficient, didn't make much mess, and she oversalted things the way Davey liked.

The new sous chef from Edinburgh, Stuart, had a degree in food engineering and had done a pastry course in Paris. He was stepping in as a favour to Massimo. He brought his own knife set, all beautiful Japanese blades. He wouldn't let Davey wash them with the other knives. At the end of his first day, he pulled Davey aside.

Look, Stuart said, I know you've got a bit of a history, and I don't judge you for it. I've worked with people like you before. I can see you're a hard worker. But if you try anything, anything at all, you're out, ok? I'm keeping an eye on you. As I say though, don't worry about it, I won't tell anyone. And, he winked, I'm not going to ask you who knocked out your front teeth, eh? Bet the other guy regrets getting on the wrong side of you. But don't let me hear about anything like that while I'm here.

Pandora's Apron

Pandora was a descendant of Lord Kelvin, after whom the river, station, park, and museum were named. She was penniless and sighed often. She'd had to turn to waitressing because things were desperate. When things were bad with her on/off boyfriend Andrew, she slept with Duncan, and complained that Andrew was boring and bourgeois and lazy. When things were going well with Andrew, she told Duncan that she was so relieved that they could be friends and colleagues without things being awkward between them. She was doing Fine Art at Glasgow School of Art and had helped Massimo choose new furnishings for improving the customer experience. He was going to propose them to head office.

Customer experience, she snorted. What bollocks. They can afford new sofas and we're on the minimum wage? And someone keeps stealing the tips. It's an outrage. If I told Dad how much we're being exploited he'd go nuts.

Massimo overheard her.

A month later, after being given only four hours work a week, Pandora accused Massimo, in the middle of lunchtime service, and in front of customers and staff alike, of trying to starve her out of work, and force her to quit, because he couldn't be bothered to fire her.

He denied it, and tried to laugh off her accusation, telling her to keep it down, and shrugging at the customers with a helpless smile. She persisted. Was he or was he not trying to get rid of her? Like a cowardly boyfriend who forces the woman to break up with them?

He told her she wasn't getting shifts because she was a lazy student who didn't pull her weight. He told her she could leave right now, if she wanted, but not to hold up the lunch rush any longer.

The customers, forks halfway to mouths, watched. The staff, running back and forth with plates, stared.

She pointed at each of the tables of staring customers and said, you are my witnesses. Don't let him get away with it. Refuse to pay your bill. Boycott this bar. We're on zero-hour contracts on the minimum wage, and our boss – who probably steals our tips by the way (Davey looked at the floor and dug his hands deep in his pockets but no one noticed) – is trying to starve me out of my job by only paying me for four hours work a week. Could any of you pay your rent on that?

The customers were silent. Massimo was furious. He didn't decide the wages and would never steal money from his staff. What power did he have? He was only a manager. It was the same everywhere and he did his best. They were like a family. If anything, she was probably the one stealing the tips.

Pandora removed her apron, threw it at his feet and said, fuck you. She walked out.

The following week she got a job as a design consultant at her cousin's firm.

Or perhaps she simply stopped turning up for shifts when she realised they were being cut. In any case, she got the consultancy job, and told her new colleagues that she felt sorry for the people who worked under those exploitative conditions. But there wasn't anything she could do about it. Still, it was sad. She'd managed to get out and she was penniless. How hard could it be? The others would quit too if they really wanted to leave.

Zero Gravity Paradise

When it happened, people were thinking about how it was a miracle, or a bomb, or that they'd had too much to drink, or possibly all three. Or they thought they were drunk until they realised everyone else knew it was happening too, and then, many of the fans were religious one way or another, so then they'd be leaning towards miracles, but also lots of people were paranoid about terrorism, so would be leaning towards thinking it was a bomb. In any case Astrid didn't think it was any of those things, but thought that other people would think it was one or some of those things.

As a waitress, she was one of the only people at the match that was more sober than sober, because she was surrounded by people who were not sober. She was thinking about the film *Thor 2: The Dark World*. It was not a good film, and she had known that when she watched the first one, which didn't stop her from watching the sequel. *Thor 2* was a Marvel superhero movie and although it was inspired by Norse mythology, the film really had nothing to do with accurately representing myths, if that's possible, or at least the myths in the film were more myths of American exceptionalism than Scandinavian pantheons. But she felt, being half Norwegian and called Astrid, she ought to take an interest in her cultural heritage anyway, that she should watch the Thor films, so she did.

In *Thor 2* the galaxies are aligning, and for a brief moment, when they align, this demonic alien (because there are aliens in these films) will open a portal that reaches across all the galaxies simultaneously. He will do something horrible with the portal (she can't remember what) and the mission is to stop this from happening, because if this giant portal opens then – and this was her favourite quote of all time – 'physics will go ballistic.' Best worst line in any film ever. What did it mean? Did it mean anything? Did language go ballistic in that line? It meant the special effects team could go wild with their budget. It meant that there was no chance Astrid would learn about Norse culture from the franchise. Which was ok because she wasn't really half Norwegian, she just had blonde actor parents who felt that if they gave their baby an unusual name then she would get ahead in life and do better than they did, because they worked in Homebase. Economics did not go ballistic for anyone in their family, and now Astrid worked for Paradise as a waitress.

Paradise was made of breezeblocks, steel and concrete. It stank of Bovril, sweat, men, and alcohol. She worked too many days a week for the minimum wage on a zero hour contract. She served five course meals in the private boxes. Then it was the first half (no alcohol). Then it was half-time (lots of alcohol), and then it was the second half (no alcohol). Corporate people probably, she didn't ask. Nearly all Scottish men. And one day, during the second half, while she was serving soft drinks, mostly tea, coffee and Irn Bru, physics went ballistic.

She was looking at the pitch, because everyone was shouting, which usually meant that something seemed like it was about to happen, but was quite likely to not happen. The ball went up. And it went up. And it did not come back down.

The shift had begun the way that all the shifts began, with Paradise looming over her like a tombstone as she approached, blotting out the sun. She tucked her shirt into her trousers, did up the top button on her shirt, and her cuffs, and put on her tie. They queued to sign in, and one boy looked at all the white shirts and black trousers and said it was like The March of the Penguins and laughed, and no one laughed with him.

She was allocated a box, signed in, and went through to the box, where the supervisor briefed them and boasted about the VIP guests that she had never heard of while everybody looked at their phones. Then he told them there was a no devices policy and slowly, with big sighs, they pocketed their phones. Then he assigned them tables, and they stood behind the top chair of their table and asked the customers about their dietary requirements (they usually didn't have any and the vegetarian option was always the same). She shook out napkins onto the laps of each guest. It was an invasion of personal space that felt as keen to her as if one of them had just tongued her ear, which one of them had done once, and she was reprimanded for screaming, though she would have done more than scream had she not held back. She would have cut out his tongue and it would have been not just his tongue, but the tongue of everyone in there, that one tongue would belong to all the guests and supervisors and all the penguins too – but she didn't cut his tongue out because that's just not something that people do.

Drinks orders were taken. One of the new waiters dropped a tray loaded with full pints of Tennent's. The boy who had said the thing about the penguins nudged her and pointed at the smashed glass, and the new waiter patting red-faced at the customer's trouser legs, looking like maybe crying would happen. Ha, the boy said. Same shit, different week. Astrid had not worked with this guy before, this guy who thought she looked like a penguin. She did not like him and suspected that unlike her, his name was boring, like James maybe, or Tim, and that his cultural heritage was authentic. She guessed that his superior amusement meant that he didn't really need to be there the way some of them really needed to be there. Duncan, he said, offering his hand. Astrid said hello and walked away with her tray of soft drinks. He was wrong to say same shit, different day. Because although it was a different day, things were not the same. As she looked at the pitch, a tray of soft drinks in one hand, the ball went up and did not come back down. It stayed up. The crowd roared, and then the roar changed, and it was unlike the roar of a goal, or the outrage of a miss, or of a yellow card, or the hitting-the-goal-post anguish, or the disbelief when something that half the crowd does not want to happen actually happens even though they don't want it to happen. It was a strange and strangled roar of unknowing, and knowing that they were seeing something that was maybe a miracle or a case of mass delusion, or at least some kind of unprecedented phenomenon that was yet to be named and would definitely be on the news on TV.

The ball went up, stayed up, and then carried on going up, until it was level with her face up in the private box, and then higher up and up until – but she stopped looking at the ball because the soft drinks she was carrying lifted off the surface of her tray. And the players on the pitch, yelling and screaming, were ascending too. There was no logic to it, such as lighter things going up first, and then heavier things. It was random as far as she could tell, and she wasn't really looking for logic anyway because there was a rending sound that jarred her teeth and bones and that sounded like how a bomb might sound in slow motion. Or underwater. And up she went too, in a kind of strange movement like being pulled upwards through water perhaps, if water wasn't so heavy. She pulled herself along the ceiling of the box, towards the fire exit, and clung there to the door frame looking out at the sky, and then looking in at all the people crashing together on the ceiling like angry balloons. The supervisor at the other end of the box yelled for her to come back.

She let go of the door frame. The cold air shushed about her as she floated up past the concrete walls of the stadium, until she was above it, and above Homebase, there in the distance. The stadium was like a little grey and green oval beneath her, an egg instead of a tombstone, and the slow motion bomb sound was cracks running around the edges as the whole building uprooted itself. She could see the city with little people, plucked upwards, rising out of the streets or clinging to ascending lamp posts. There was the cathedral, and clouds of dust at the edge of the city, where little wind turbines, buried deep, rose too. She was ascending slowly now, ecstatic. She undid her cuffs, her top button, removed her tie, and kicked off her shoes, which did not fall towards Paradise, but hovered there beneath her. Astrid turned to face the sky where the sun blazed cold above the clouds –

Night Shift

4am, black shirts line up under artificial lights, sign the time sheet. Black shoes stick and unstick, mint leaves, Bacardi, Laurent Perrier. A single earring lies under a chair. Then alone crossing the river. The BBC Scotland building rises up ahead. The sky fades from pink to blue, shades of eggshell in the glass buildings along the opposite bank, and in the water, which also holds half the moon.

11th June
Orange peel on concrete.

15th June
Crossing the cranes of Clydebank another her with another crane unfolds the origami of possibilities. He knows what he wants, he knows not, I want that/to know, I don't.

16th June
A woman gets out of a car, a man in the passenger's seat. She has one red heel on, one Converse, and climbs over the wall into the estate.

19th June
Finished early, BBC Scotland building still lit up, light reflected on the river, on fire, melting and bending from right to left as she crosses the bridge. Further up, flowers spill over the estate wall, in the streetlight you can't tell if they're white or yellow. Camellias or roses, maybe something else, never look at them in the day. The fuchsias are covering their purple skirts to reveal them later. A Saltire flag as a curtain, thin enough to see through to the bare walls and bright, naked bulb.

22nd June
Just the look of windscreens and concrete in the rain. Fool's gold.

23rd June

Rain, a cardboard Tennent's box umbrella. An upstairs kitchen light; a half-naked woman bends down over the counter.

24th June

Broken glass on the sofas, wet. They crowded around the canapés, snatched handfuls, left half eaten fish cakes on the tables, floor. Danced on furniture, the hostess once a mother, always a mother, picked ribbons and cake off the floor. Music loud, tomorrow's money jumped up and down in black and white, mocktails in hand. Over two grand. Happy twelfth birthday.

25th June

3am on Glasgow Green, on a bench with a bottle of Blossom Hill on a Sunday night. Duncan smokes for the first time, says he has the urge to drive. An Estonian comes over and talks about his job in the Hilton. Ewelina had a garden with plum trees once.

Acknowledgements

I would like to thank those who published earlier versions of these stories in *Adjacent Pineapple*, *Box[Ed.]*, *Dear Green Place*, *SPAM* zine, and *An Unofficial Apprentice Poetry Anthology* (SPAM Press), *Streetcake* and *The King of Birds* (Hickathrift Press). I would also like to thank the Victoria Writer's Circle, Marine Furet, Katherine Thomas, Caitlin Stobie, and Lila Matsumoto for their support in developing these stories. Thank you to Aaron Kent and the Broken Sleep Books team for all their work on this book and for bringing *Zero Hours* to life.

Thank you to Jen Calleja, Ruby Cowling, and Fernando Sdrigotti for their lovely words about this book and Fernando Sdrigotti for publishing an excerpt in minor literature[s]

I would like to thank Katrina Falco for her gorgeous cover design, my family for encouraging me to keep writing, and Greg, for everything.

LAY OUT YOUR UNREST

Ingram Content Group UK Ltd.
Milton Keynes UK
UKHW041336090723
424797UK00004B/204

9 781915 079503